RERUNS

STORIES BY
PATRICK IRELAN

Patrick Irelan

icp books
north liberty, iowa

RERUNS—STORIES BY PATRICK IRELAN

Copyright © 2009 Patrick Irelan

ISBN 9781888160406

Library of Congress Control Number: 2008943257

Ice Cube Press (est. 1993)
205 North Front Street
North Liberty, Iowa 52317-9302
www.icecubepress.com
steve@icecubepress.com

Printed in Canada

The paper used in this publication meets the minimum requirements of
the American National Standard for Information Sciences—Permanence
of Paper for Printed Library Materials, ANSI Z39.48-1992

Many of these stories first appeared in literary journals and anthologies—
"Reruns" and "No-Name Place" in *Opium Magazine*; "Comets" in *Prairie
Weather*; "Never Carnal" in *Kansas Quarterly*; "New Zealand New" in
Bravado; "Dark Matter" in *Iowa City Magazine*; "The Band That Be-
guiles" in *Whiskey Island*; "Bar Biscuits" in *Uncle*; and "Self-Starter" in the
DeKalb Literary Arts Journal. "Minutes" and "Patrick Noland: His Life and
Work" appeared online at *Amazon Shorts* and *Pindeldyboz*, respectively.

Cover photo credit: LC-USW3-015449-E DLC (b&w film nitrate neg.)

To Janet

I have travelled a good deal in Concord; and every where, in shops, and offices, and fields, the inhabitants have appeared to me to be doing penance in a thousand remarkable ways.
—Henry David Thoreau

CONTENTS

RERUNS

I FLY ON A MISSION of peace to the troubled island nation of Kadoo
Royale. The stewardess gives me peanuts, cashews, almonds, macadamia
nuts, tiny bottles of gin, coffee with nondairy creamer, the *Critique of
Pure Reason*. She says to call her whenever I need her. I am the only passenger. I call her many times.

We arrive at nightfall. I kiss the stewardess and shake hands with the
pilot and copilot. They will refuel and leave at once. I will be the only
American left on Kadoo Royale.

President Yutter meets me on the tarmac, and I present my card:

> Patrick Rialto
> Department of State
> Washington, DC 20520
> Phone 1-800-END-WARS

"Welcome to our troubled island nation," says the president, speaking
through an interpreter.

"I come on a mission of peace," I reply. We embrace in the glare of
television lights, even though there is no television station anywhere
near Kadoo Royale.

On the long drive to the city he reviews the island's violent past. Two
rival factions have fought for control of the nation for more than two
hundred years. The members of both groups trace their ancestry to the
same party of colonists from northern Europe. Both groups failed to

see at the outset that there was nothing of value on Kadoo Royale. Now they compete for the island's only source of foreign currency, the production and sale of postage stamps.

In spite of their animosity, the members of the two groups are almost identical. They all have fair skin. They practice the same religion. They speak the same language. No one remembers the original cause of their rivalry.

The only apparent difference between the two factions involves the name of the island itself. One group pronounces it "Kadoo Royale," and the other calls it "Kadöo Royale." President Yutter says, "No one knows how many lives have been lost to this issue."

A message awaits me at the guest house in Yutterburg. My Kadoovian undercover contact bids me welcome. His code name: Mangrove.

Next morning, the peace conference begins.

As chief arbitrator, I deliver the opening remarks, stressing the importance of our mission. "Ladies and Gentlemen," I say, "we have before us an opportunity to bring peace to your land, a peace that will last for generations. We must put to rest old rivalries, old hatreds, and old misunderstandings. The people want it. They demand it. We must not fail."

I pause for dramatic effect. My gray eyes survey the crowd. My blue suit and silk tie denote wealth and power. "If we succeed in our quest for peace, I can promise you the continued support of my country. I can promise you food. I can promise hair dryers. I promise silicon, integrated circuits, BHT, group dynamics, structuralism, and poststructuralism." My voice rises. "I promise conceptual art!"

I wait for applause, but all I get is silence. I look around for an explanation. Then I see the problem. The interpreter has not yet arrived.

Twenty minutes later, the interpreter finally enters the hall. I repeat my opening remarks, and the real work of the conference gets underway. The delegates begin by arguing over lemon- or lime-flavored mineral water. I suggest unflavored mineral water. The delegates grumble but agree.

We move on to other matters. Both sides state their demands and refuse to compromise. Both sides want blue jeans, digital watches, a television station. I make a list. "The Kadoos always get what they want," shouts one delegate. "The Kadöos always try to run everything," shouts another. The talks have reached an impasse. I announce a recess until tomorrow morning.

I leave the conference hall and walk through the streets of the city, looking for insights into the character of the people. I must find the basis for an historic compromise. On a street corner I see a vending machine with the island's only newspaper: *USA Today*. On the next corner a man is selling Reeboks and frozen yogurt.

I observe the people as they pass by—their smooth white skin; their alert blue eyes; their innocent faces, hungry for mega-malls and MTV. They have strong, well-formed limbs. They speak quickly and laugh often. Their souls cry out for peace.

I walk back to the guest house, my mind seething. Inside, the maid is making the bed. I stare at her firm, young body. She stares at my rugged face. I smile. She takes off her clothes.

We fall into bed, and I escape the frustrations of diplomacy. The maid has breasts like melons and legs like a goddess. Her eyes are deep pools. Her name is Yes-Yes.

Afterwards, we lie in bed, talking of love. My interpreter explains that Yes-Yes is a Kadoo. I am careful not to speak *mit Umlaut*. We talk far into the night.

The next morning, a message is waiting in my mailbox. Every house on the island has a mailbox, despite the fact that Kadoo Royale does not have a postal service. Mangrove has sent his first substantive communication: RETURN TO SENDER.

I ponder this message as I ride to the conference with President Yutter in his 1953 Studebaker. After reaching the hall, I mount the podium and gavel the delegates into silence. I must take command if I am to achieve my goal: a fair and honorable peace for both Kadoos and Kadöos.

The first speaker is Tex Beneke Yutter, leader of the Kadoos. "For too long," he says in a stentorian voice, "the Kadöos have retained control of the Philatelic Sales Division. We demand parity for Kadoos!"

Pandemonium breaks out in the hall. I pound the gavel, but to no avail. Everyone wants to speak at once. Finally, I turn off the lights and the noise stops. I turn the lights back on. Everyone is asleep.

After a break for coffee and croissants, the session resumes with a speech by Artie Shaw Yutter, the leader of the Kadöos. "The Kadoos demand parity," he says, "but they're unwilling to work for it. They want everything given to them."

A howl of protest greets these words. Delegates exchange threats. Push comes to shove. Objects fly through the air: pens, pencils, chairs, bottles of unflavored mineral water. The talks have again reached an impasse. I announce an early adjournment and run for the Studebaker.

I reach the safety of the guest house, where Yes-Yes awaits me. She massages my neck and shoulders to calm my spirit. She removes my shirt and smoothes my skin with coconut oil and guar gum. I fall asleep. In my dream Tex Beneke Yutter and Artie Shaw Yutter are dueling with rolled copies of *USA Today*.

When I awake, dinner is ready. Yes-Yes has prepared a meal of squid, Hamburger Helper, and partially hydrogenated vegetable oil. After dinner we share a bottle of bulk-process champagne. I stare at Yes-Yes. She is beautiful in her colorful native garb. She removes her clothes, and I remove mine. Her skin is the color of ivory. Mine is the color of peeled bananas.

We hurry to bed, and I tell her I love her. I tell her I will always love her. I tell her I have never loved anyone else. At a crucial moment, a loud noise interrupts our progress. The interpreter has fallen off his chair.

Afterwards, I check the mailbox, where I find another note from Mangrove: GO FISH.

I leave immediately for Washington. The same crew is on the plane. The stewardess gives me a case of gin, a bucketful of Brazil nuts, and *Being and Nothingness*. We lie down in the aisle. I am glad to be rid of the interpreter.

The secretary of state confers with me as soon as I arrive in Washington. I struggle to explain the nature of the conflict and the importance of the Philatelic Sales Division in a country without a post office.

"You must forge a compromise," he says.

"I understand," I reply.

"Be imaginative."

"I try."

"Be diplomatic."

"Of course."

"Promise them something."

"I have."

"Promise them something else. Promise them CDs, DVDs, flat-screen television, roller derby, canasta, fiber optics, electronic scoreboards. Don't be timid."

Suddenly, I see his point. The man is brilliant, a genius. His eyebrows meet above his nose. "Yes," I say. "Of course, of course."

While stateside, I visit my family in Reston, VA 22070. I embrace my wife, Teri, and my children, Bobbi, Billie, Toni, Patti, Randi, Mindi, Willie, Traci, Sandi, and Cindi. I love my family more than life itself. I leave at once for the airport.

Back on board, the stewardess rips off my clothes. We cruise at thirty thousand feet.

The plane lands at three in the morning. President Yutter is waiting in the Studebaker. I have sometimes wondered why the president doesn't have a chauffeur, but have decided I shouldn't ask. He's an excellent driver himself, though too short to see over the top of the steering wheel.

As he drives away from the airport, President Yutter begins to talk excitedly. He pauses for the translation, and we hear the interpreter snoring in the back seat. The president stops the car, wakens the man with a kick, and repeats himself.

"You have returned just in time for Founder's Day," he says. "It is our most important national holiday. It commemorates the day two hundred years ago when John Paul Jones Yutter founded the Philatelic Sales Division."

"Fascinating," I say. "I've been meaning to ask, what is the Philatelic Sales Division a division of?"

"The founder originally planned to establish a post office department."

"Yes."

"But he found this impractical in a country where everyone is named Yutter."

"I see."

"So Philatelic Sales isn't really a division of anything. It is its own *raison d'être.*"

We arrive in Yutterburg at dawn. I would like to see Yes-Yes, but the president insists on finding a good spot for the parade. After standing in the sun for six hours, we finally hear the sound of a marching band. By this time, the crowd is ten or twelve deep on both sides of the parade route. A cheer goes up as the music gets louder.

As the band comes into view, I see that it consists entirely of one man with a boom box. His purple uniform is immaculate. A limousine with bulletproof glass follows directly behind him. The limo contains only one passenger, an imposing figure of a man with an ostrich feather in his hat and a wide sash running diagonally across his chest. His face is rigid. His lip curls. He looks as if he would gladly pull your head off. President Yutter, his voice cracking with emotion, explains that this is the director of the Philatelic Sales Division: Donald Trump Yutter.

The noise from the crowd rises to a deafening roar. As the limousine rolls on down the street, I turn to watch the rest of the parade. I'm surprised to see that the crowd is breaking up. The parade is over. I turn back toward President Yutter. Tears are streaming down his face. He cannot speak. I lend him my handkerchief, and we head for the Studebaker.

After lunch we spend an hour finding the interpreter. Then the president takes me for a tour of the city. He begins by driving past the headquarters of the Philatelic Sales Division, a massive six-story building made of Indiana limestone. A statue of John Paul Jones Yutter stands atop a stamp machine in the front lawn. Soldiers armed with M-16 rifles guard the building.

Following this glimpse of Philatelic Sales, the president parks in the next block to give me a closer look at the other governmental entities, all of which reside in Yutterburg's unfinished post office. President Yutter's desk stands next to the stamp window, where he spends his time telling people to go away.

We climb back into the car and drive another block to the city's retail center—a Wal-Mart that sells hundreds of products: food, clothing, furniture, used Studebakers. We pause for a snack of Fritos and Diet Pepsi.

Having completed our tour of the downtown, we drive to a typical residential neighborhood. The yards are small but tidy. Children are playing on the sidewalks. We park the car and walk up to a house, which like all houses in the city is constructed of particle board.

A smiling householder meets us at the door. His face and those of his wife and children cry out for peace. He shows us into the living room, which contains a chair and a color television set. As the honored guest, I sit on the chair while the others stand. This is my chance to enter the hearts and minds of these simple folk.

"Your faces cry out for peace," I say. "What will bring peace to you simple folk?"

"*I Love Lucy* reruns," says the woman.

"Game shows," says the man.

The children pick their noses and pee on the floor.

"We've tried for decades to get a television station," says President Yutter, "but no one will help us."

"I see, I see." I nod my head wisely. "I believe that peace will come."

I shake hands with the man and woman, but not with the children. President Yutter leads the way back to the car. After a long day together, we have become friends. On the way to the guest house, he confides to me that he prefers *Gunsmoke* to *I Love Lucy*. I promise never to tell.

As I climb out of the Studebaker in front of the guest house, I remind the president to pick me up in the morning on his way to the peace conference. That's when he tells me the conference will not meet in the morning. On Kadoo Royale, Founder's Day lasts for a month.

Faced with a month of inactivity, I decide to spend the time constructively at the Yutter Memorial Library. I arrive early next morning, only to find that my interpreter has disappeared somewhere along the way.

After taking an hour to find him, I return to the library, where I delve into the fascinating history and geography of Kadoo Royale. I learn that the island is roughly circular, with a diameter of approximately fifty miles. It contains no rivers or lakes. The terrain consists entirely of rock. Everything used on the island has to be imported—dirt, water, glue—everything.

Since nothing grows on the island, there is no cultivation and no peasantry. Almost everyone lives in Yutterburg, the country's only city, which is located on the northern coast. In an earlier attempt to populate other areas, the Philatelic Sales Division constructed an airport on the southern coast and built a highway along the shore to connect it with the city. Unfortunately, no one wants to work at an airport that receives just one flight per week.

The only people who don't live in the city are the members of the island's small aboriginal tribe. The aborigines move from place to place, stealing whatever they need from the Kadoos and Kadöos. No one knows how they supported themselves before the arrival of the colonists. They have resisted all efforts to assimilate them, and they have no interest in professional wrestling.

At last, Founder's Day reaches its conclusion. Armed with my newly acquired knowledge, I reconvene the peace conference. "Ladies and gentlemen," I say, "throughout your long history, you have overcome many problems together. Both Kadoos and Kadöos have contributed greatly to the success of your nation. I urge you to bear that in mind as we continue our search for peace. Now is the time to remember your common history. Now is the time to rebuild your country. Now is the time for all Kadoovians to put aside old rivalries and dedicate themselves to one nation—Kadoo Royale!"

The delegates leap to their feet and sing the Kadoo Royale national anthem, "The Yellow Rose of Texas." Tears come to my eyes as I see the delegates united for the first time. They sing the anthem again, and I soak my handkerchief.

The singing ends, the delegates sit down, and the first speaker, a Kadoo, walks to the podium. "In this new spirit of brotherhood," he says, "I call upon the Kadöos to share control of the Philatelic Sales Division. All citizens should have equal access to the most valuable stamps."

Instantly, a Kadöo jumps to his feet. "When you Kadoos ran the Philatelic Sales Division, you forgot to use perforated paper," he shouts.

"What about the time the Kadöos printed the stamps on the same side with the glue?" shouts another delegate.

Chaos fills the hall. I call for order, but no one hears me. Fights break out. Someone sets fire to the podium. Once again I am forced to flee for my life.

The uproar that started in the conference hall spreads to the streets. With civil war now likely, I cable Washington to request emergency assistance. Thirty minutes later, I receive a note from Mangrove: WIN ONE FOR THE GIPPER.

%

That evening, I stand on the roof of the guest house. Smoke is rising from fires all over the city. I hear shouts, sirens, small-arms fire. Stripped of its contents, the Wal-Mart is burning like a marshmallow.

Suddenly, I see something on the horizon. Tiny black dots are approaching. As the dots come closer, I see that there are dozens of them, maybe hundreds. They come even closer, and I can tell that they're exactly what I've been waiting for—helicopters, hundreds of them.

They reach the city and start to descend. All around me, helicopters are floating down like soap bubbles. As each bubble touches the ground, a door pops open and out jumps a Dallas Cowboys cheerleader. Hundreds of gorgeous cheerleaders hop out of their bubbles, bringing with them the promise of America: straight teeth, perfect hair, one-stop shopping.

As the bubbles continue to land, the people of Kadoo Royale drop their stones and clubs, their gasoline bombs, their Wal-Mart loot. They watch the miracle of the bubbles, their eyes filled with wonder, their faces alive with joy.

The whole nation stands transfixed as the cheerleaders bounce through the crowds of people, giving away DVDs, satellite dishes, video games, cable TV, assault rifles, light-emitting diodes, logical positivism.

After distributing their gifts, the cheerleaders teach the Kadoovians how to memorize long lists of words and numbers. They deliver subliminal messages to free them from their doubts and anxieties, thereby helping them realize their full potential. They contribute to the relief of disasters that have not yet happened. They erect computer-operated scoreboards and teach the people rudimentary cheers.

Freed of their doubts and anxieties, the Kadoovians go into a collective swoon. Their blue eyes turn up in their noble heads. They forget their hatred for each other and begin singing advertising jingles for long-distance telephone companies. They join hands in a human chain that reaches all the way from the coastal highway to the Philatelic Sales Division, where the director announces a new issue to commemorate the occasion. The people fire their assault rifles into the air in celebration. My mission of peace has come to an end.

The grateful people of Kadoo Royale organize a farewell celebration in my honor. A convoy of fifty Studebakers sets out for the airport, with me, Yes-Yes, and the interpreter riding at the head of the procession with President Yutter. I know that Yes-Yes is sick with grief over my departure, and I try to console her.

The convoy heads out of the city amidst great rejoicing. People line the streets, cheering wildly and waving American flags. The drivers honk their horns, blink their lights, and throw Hostess Twinkies to the children. But once out of the city, the drive takes longer than the celebrants expected, and about half the drivers turn back to avoid missing the day's *Bonanza* rerun. A few miles later another bunch starts back to catch *The Beverly Hillbillies*. By the time we get to the airport, our car is the only one left, and President Yutter is eager to get home in time for *Green Acres*.

To preserve my country's dignity, I insist that the president must stay long enough to hear my farewell address. I stand in front of the airport terminal and begin to read from my prepared remarks. President Yutter shakes his head and waves his arms, and I soon understand why. Once again, the interpreter has vanished.

I've finally lost all patience with this interpreter. He's the most unprofessional man I've ever worked with. The next time I come to Kadoo Royale I'll demand someone else. I look around for him in hopes of salvaging something from my speech. Suddenly, I see him ducking into the abandoned Holiday Inn across the street, hand in hand with Yes-Yes.

For my part, this spoils the ceremony. It also explains why the interpreter was always missing when I needed him. I have no interest now in finishing my speech, to the clear relief of President Yutter, who hops into his Studebaker and roars off for *Green Acres*.

All this has dampened my spirits, but I console myself with the knowledge of what awaits me in the airplane parked at Gate 1. I hurry through the terminal and onto the plane, where the stewardess sets me down, fastens my seat belt, and tells me she's pregnant.

"I'm much too sick to roll around in the aisle with you," she says. "Besides that, it isn't safe. I have to think about the baby. And by the way, I need some money. I can't pay all these medical bills myself, and my health insurance is practically worthless, so you're going to have to start taking up the slack. And that reminds me, I have someone redecorating the baby's room. I had to move into a bigger house, of course, but the baby's room just wasn't right. So how soon can you get me some cash? These people like to get paid right away, you know."

The stewardess sits down, fastens her seat belt, and falls asleep. She doesn't show me how to use the oxygen mask. She doesn't point out the nearest exit. She doesn't tell me how to use the seat cushion as a flotation device.

Two hours later she wakes up, pushes a cart down the aisle, and dumps a cold roast-beef sandwich into my lap. I remove the tinfoil and find a piece of paper sticking out of the bun. It bears my last communication from Mangrove: HAVE ELOPED WITH YOUR WIFE. THANKS FOR FLYING THE FRIENDLY SKIES.

COMETS

MARV SCANNED THE HEAVENS with his binoculars. Venus, the Big Dipper, the North Star, the Little Dipper, the red light on top of the water tower. All this was fine, but he was looking for something else, something more important.

He heard the back door open behind him. "Marv," said a woman's voice. "Marv."

"Yeah?" He lowered the binoculars.

"What're you doing out there?"

"Looking for comets."

There was a short pause. "Comets?"

"Yeah."

"Come inside, Marv."

"All right, all right." He lifted the binoculars to his eyes, and the door closed. Fay didn't know about comets. He'd explain later, but for now he was busy. He surveyed the sky again. Mars, the Milky Way, the brief flare of a meteor, one of the four clocks on the courthouse bell tower. But no comets, none that he could see, that is. He wasn't sure where to look.

He decided to take a more methodical approach. Starting in the south, he swept the binoculars across the sky from east to west and west to east. He did this again and again, a little higher each time.

After a few minutes, his neck began to hurt. He lowered the binoculars. This wasn't what he'd hoped for. Perhaps he should've read the entire article. He turned and walked back to the house.

"What were you doing out there?" Fay said.

"I told you," Marv said, "looking for comets." He sat down at the kitchen table and picked up the newspaper.

"There's no comets tonight," she said. "I haven't heard anything about comets."

"These scientists think there's comets every night," Marv said, "all year long."

"Let me see." She walked up behind him and looked over his shoulder. He was right, at least in part. Some space scientists had suggested that millions of small comets made of snow entered the earth's atmosphere every year, thereby explaining the origins of the oceans and all the rest of the water on the planet. "But look," Fay said, pointing at a paragraph. "You can't see them with binoculars. The only way to see them is with cameras on earth satellites or with big telescopes, and even then you can't be sure what you're seeing."

Marv closed the newspaper. Fay always saw the details but missed the main point.

"They're not the big comets that have long tails," she said. "They're just little ones."

Now she has to keep talking about it, Marv thought. She can't just let it drop. "Okay," he said. "You're right. I see what you mean." He climbed the stairs to their dark bedroom, raised a window shade, and looked up at the sky.

The next morning, Marv was trying to attach a new hose to one of the sprayers when a Ford sedan covered with gravel dust pulled up beneath the hand-painted sign: MARV'S QUICK-CLEAN CARWASH. The driver wore dark glasses, a dark mustache, and dark hair. He ignored the "Closed" sign, stuck his head out the window, and said, "Are you open?"

"No," Marv said. "I wish I was, but I'm not." He walked over to the car, wiping his hands on a rag. "The city won't let me use any more water." He folded the rag and wiped the sweat from his forehead.

"Damn," the man said. "My wife wants the car washed."

"They're still letting them water the greens at the golf course. You might drive out and park beside one of the sprinklers."

The man looked at him for a moment as if this were a serious idea. "When're you going to open up again?" he finally said.

"Whenever it starts raining again," Marv said, gesturing vaguely at the sky, "if it ever does. Or whenever the city says I can use the water." The man looked at him without saying anything else, then backed out and drove away.

Marv went back to the hose. He attached it to the sprayer, slid the clamp into place, and tightened the screw. He gave the screw an extra turn for good measure, gave it one more, and stripped the threads.

"Shit!" he said. "Shit, shit, shit." He threw the screwdriver on the floor and kicked it. It flew out the door and rattled into a storm sewer. Marv's arms and shoulders went limp. "What the hell?" he said. "What difference does it make?"

He locked the doors and climbed into the pickup. On the way home, he went out of his way to drive past the golf course. He didn't see any dirty cars on the greens.

Fay put their lunch on the table, sat down, and helped herself. When Marv made no attempt to reach the serving bowls, she pushed them across the table until they formed a little barricade between them.

"I'm not hungry," he said.

"You'd better eat something," she said. "You're already losing weight. I can tell from your clothes. You have to eat if you're going to keep your strength up."

Marv thought this was an odd statement, coming from Fay. Her arms and legs were as bony as a kangaroo's, but she couldn't jump over a crack in the sidewalk. Marv knew he wasn't in great shape either, but at least he didn't look like a kangaroo. He spooned a little of everything onto his plate. "The only thing that's going to keep my strength up is rain ... or something."

"Something? You mean comets?"

Marv nibbled at a piece of ham. "I mean something. Anything." He took a tiny bite of potato salad.

"I read the rest of that article. That comet idea is only a theory. It hasn't been proven. And even if it was true, it wouldn't fill the reservoir."

"It's only a theory, but it's a good theory, and I didn't say it would fill the reservoir."

Fay cut a piece of ham, shoved it into her mouth, and chewed vigorously. Even her long face looked like a kangaroo's. "Maybe what we should do is move somewhere—California or Texas or someplace where you could get a job. It's never going to get any better in these little Iowa towns, even if it does rain."

Marv put his fork down and pushed his plate up against the barricade. "I don't want to move," he said.

"Why not?" said Fay before taking another bite.

"Because this is where I belong. My family has lived here a hundred and sixty years."

"You're living in the past. People don't stay in the same place their whole lives anymore. They move around all the time."

"I know, but that's just it. I don't want to move around all the time."

Fay helped herself to some more potato salad. "I know you don't," she said. "That's the problem."

Marv stood up and walked outside.

Ten minutes later, he stuck his head in the back door and said he was going fishing. He made a noisy production of getting his fishing gear into the back of the pickup. A rod and reel. A coffee can full of dirt and night crawlers. A tackle box full of hooks, lures, sinkers, bobbers, and a jumble of other stuff. Then another rod and reel.

He piled all this in and drove off down the street. When he got to the reservoir, he parked under a big maple tree and looked out at the water, what there was left of it. Two of the three intake pipes were sticking up out of the water, and the third was just inches below the surface. When the reservoir fell below the level of the last intake pipe, no one knew where the town would get more water. The city council was still arguing about it.

Marv opened the glove compartment and pulled out a bottle of bourbon. He took two swigs, exhaled loudly, and took another. Each drink tasted better than the one before.

Feeling a little better, he put the bottle away and looked out at the water again. His grandfather had helped build this reservoir during the drought of the 1930's. The WPA funded the project. Marv's grandfather brought his mules to work every day for five months, receiving his pay in surplus wheat. Marv wondered if there was still a surplus.

He took out his handkerchief and wiped the sweat from his face and neck. He didn't understand how it could be so humid and still not rain. He started the pickup, drove back into town, and parked in front of a small brick building with a red-tile roof. The word "Carnegie" was engraved in a block of limestone above the door.

Marv hadn't been inside the building for years. He had no idea where to look, so he went straight to the librarian—a young woman he'd never seen before. She helped him find a book and a couple of magazine articles, and he sat down at a corner table. He was glad the library was air-conditioned.

He stayed at the table for two hours. During that time he learned more about comets than he'd ever thought possible. He found that the large comets most people have seen or heard about are made of ice, frozen gases, and dust. These comets, such as the one named after Edmund Halley, periodically emerge from the distant regions of the solar system and come into view. When one of these gets close enough to the sun, its outer layers melt, creating a tail of dust and vapor. Sunlight passing through this tail can give the comet a spectacular appearance.

But far more numerous than these large comets, according to a theory first advanced in the 1980's, are the millions of small comets inhabiting the solar system. Each of these consists of snow with a coating of black dust. Each is about the size of a small house and weighs about twenty to forty tons. Approximately twenty small comets enter the earth's upper atmosphere every minute and evaporate in the sky, thereby continually adding to the planet's supply of water.

When he'd read all that he could absorb, Marv stood up and walked outside. It was still hot, but he hardly noticed. His mind was full of small comets, millions of them, hurtling through space with enough water to wash all the cars in the galaxy.

Marv's visit to the library left him feeling a little dry, so he drove back to the reservoir for some more fishing. Two hours later he pulled into his driveway, turned off the engine, took the bottle out of the glove compartment, and knocked back his last shot of the afternoon. Then he climbed out, slammed the door, hitched up his pants, and walked around the truck, kicking the tires. Reading about all those comets had given him a burst of energy. He stopped and looked at the mirror on the passenger's side. "Objects in mirror are closer than they appear," it said at the bottom. Marv looked at his reflection. His head seemed longer than usual, not like a kangaroo's, but more like an artillery shell. The top of his head formed the flat end of the shell, and his chin formed the pointed end.

He kicked the last tire, then walked into the backyard and looked across the vacant lot behind his house. In the field beyond the houses on the next street, his cousin's soybeans withered in the sun. The Lowe family wasn't having a good year.

He walked into the house, letting the screen door slam behind him. He didn't care if he woke up the mayor and the whole city council. Someone needed to. He opened the refrigerator and rattled about inside.

"Is that you, Marv?" said Fay's voice from upstairs.

"No," Marv said. "It's Guy Lombardo and the Royal Canadians."

"Well stay out of the refrigerator. I have something in the oven. It'll be ready in fifteen minutes."

Marv shut the refrigerator door and clomped into the living room. He switched on the TV, turned up the volume, and flopped down on the couch. A young woman with curly hair was pointing at the symbols on a weather map and talking as fast as she could. The map suddenly disappeared, and the woman sped through the succession of numbers that took its place. Finally, she sat down with a middle-aged man at a long desk, and both said, "No relief in sight."

Fay came downstairs just as the man began talking about the trial of two college football players who'd robbed a Quik Trip. "Why's it so loud?" she said, turning down the volume.

"I don't wanna miss anything," Marv said. "You might miss something if you can't hear it." His big feet stuck out over the end of the couch.

"Have you been drinking again?" Fay said.

"Not much," he said. "Just enough to clear my head."

"Drinking doesn't clear your head. It does just the opposite."

"Not for me. I can't make sense of anything till I've had a few. The more I drink, the more sense everything makes. If I drank enough, I could probably figure out how to run a carwash without water."

"That's nonsense, and you know it. You're just looking for an excuse to drink."

"I don't need an excuse. I drink because I want to, because I like it. I can't think of anything I'd rather do."

Fay gave him a look of revulsion and walked out of the room.

Five hours later, Marv stood alone in the darkness of the backyard, his binoculars in one hand, the bottle of bourbon in the other. Fay was in the house watching a television show about the problems of a wealthy family in southern California.

As he peered into the sky, Marv considered the possibility that at that very moment, comets made of snow were falling toward the earth: twenty comets every minute, hundreds every hour, thousands every day, and millions every year. And even though he knew that these comets, if they existed, would be invisible to him with his cheap binoculars, he suddenly found that he could see them anyway. On all sides, comets were falling toward the earth, shrinking into vapor as they entered the atmosphere.

Marv saw them, saw them all as they evaporated and formed into clouds, huge dark clouds that rolled in from the west, booming as they came. And then the rain began to fall, lightly at first, then harder and harder.

It fell on the corn and soybeans. On abandoned coal mines and deserted farms. On forgotten railroads and small towns. On towns that no longer existed.

Water collected in puddles, emptied into rivulets, and ran down to the rivers and creeks. The Fox River and the Skunk. The Whitebreast and the Wyaconda. The Cedar, the Chariton, and the Des Moines.

Water filled the lakes—Lake Wapello, Lake Icaria, and the Lake of Three Fires. It filled the reservoir, rising higher above the first intake pipe, then above the second, and then the third. Rain was falling everywhere, bringing with it the smell of dirt and hay and cars covered with gravel dust.

Marv saw all these things: the comets, the clouds, the rain, the wet fields, the rivers and lakes, and the water filling the reservoir.

He saw them, even though he knew they were invisible. And when Fay came to the back door and called him, all he could hear was the sound of the rain.

NO-NAME PLACE

On the south side of Cedar Rapids, Iowa, there exists a landscape for which there are no adjectives. For a transcendent view of this spot, one needs to drive south out of the metropolis on Interstate 380. Strangers sometimes drive innocently past houses and businesses before reaching the crest of a hill and starting down the other side. A glance to the right at this point can prove fatal. This prospect, when seen without warning, has led some motorists to commit suicide by driving off the road into an immovable object such as a bulldozer or a senator from Utah.

This spot has no name. It exists in that realm of the surreal where no name is adequate. It is bounded on the north by the crest of the hill just mentioned. On the east, the interstate highway forms the boundary. And on the south, the Union Pacific Railroad has driven back more suicidal assaults than the Union soldiers who held the sunken lane at the Battle of Shiloh. Beyond this, steam rises from the ADM corn-processing plant like smoke from England's dark satanic mills.

But to the west, the endless horizon of the west, the Los Angelization of Iowa rolls ever onward like Manifest Destiny, the course of empire, and the white-man's burden. And what a burden it is, for even the quickest glance reveals to anyone that not even God could stop it: the Clarion Hotel, the Marion Hotel, Qwik Trip, Slow Trip, Wal-Mart, Handimart, Red Lobster, White Lobster, Blue Lobster, Taco John's, Taco Jack's, Taco Jill's, Burger Chef, Best Buy, Good-Bye, Target, Forget, Super 8 Motel, Super 9 Gotel, Happy Hawkeye Truck Stop, the Cedar Valley Casino and Mortuary, and onward forever into the west.

Drivers instinctively press down on the accelerator in order to get past this affliction before it draws them into itself and devours them like a teenager swallowing a Big Mac, like a whale swallowing a teenager, like a senator from Utah swallowing a whale.

For years, for decades, No-Name Place and its western horizon has so unnerved me that I felt it necessary to consult the psychiatric division of the University of Iowa Hospitals and Clinics. "There's no getting around it, Son," Doctor X told me as I lay on his couch one spring day in the year 2020. "To defeat our fears, we must confront and confound them." Tortoise-shell frames enclosed the round lenses of his glasses. He drew deeply on his corncob pipe and filled the room with black smoke like England's dark satanic, etc.

"Doctor X," I said politely as I adjusted the pillow, "have you ever been to No-Name Place and confronted its unending western horizon?" The very thought caused me to shiver. I pulled up the blanket.

"No, Patrick, I haven't. My workload makes it impossible for me to personally test every treatment I prescribe for my patients."

I saw that I'd have to go it alone. I shivered again. "Doctor X, could I have another blanket?"

"Nurse," he shouted.

A nurse instantly appeared and threw a blanket at me. She looked like the nurses in a Mel Brooks movie. She had blond hair with billowing curls. She wore white pumps with six-inch heels and a white dress that terminated a third of the way down her thighs. A thought hit me. "Nurse," I said, "have you ever confronted—." The door slammed with such force that I couldn't hear anything for ten minutes.

After my hearing returned, Doctor X gave me a pep talk and enough prescriptions for a six-year supply of psychotropic agents. As I walked out of the office, I tried to take the blankets with me, but a guard seized them at the door. I asked him if I could borrow his assault rifle, but he said no. I felt lucky to have escaped with the pillow.

❧

I sat on the shoulder of I-380, confronting No-Name Place. I wished that I had the couch that belonged to Doctor X, but he wouldn't let me borrow it.

No-Name Place lay below the elevation of the highway. Spread out before me, a maze of concrete and asphalt streets wound its way through the heart of darkness. In the distance, the maze disappeared into the muddy sky of the horizon.

Six hours after sitting down, my body trembling from my Chicago Cubs cap to my combat boots, I stood up and walked down the exit ramp from I-380 into the maze. I would've driven my 1997 Toyota Corolla, but the police had already towed it.

As I walked through No-Name Place, using a can of spray paint, I left a trail of red arrows on the asphalt or concrete, respectively, thinking this would later help me find my way out. The place appeared to be deserted. Four hours later, I saw a man approaching. I kept my eyes on him as I bent down and sprayed an arrow. I stood up, walked on, and met the stranger in the middle of the street. He wore a Chicago White Sox cap, an Australian Army uniform, and combat boots.

"How you doing, Soldier?" I said.

"How do you get out of here?" he said.

"Follow the red arrows."

"What red arrows?"

I looked back at the red arrows. Vanished. I bent down to spray the can. Empty.

Twenty-four hours later, having spent the night at the Clarion Hotel and having eaten nothing but Big Macs, we found the red arrows and followed them up the ramp to I-380. The soldier walked away to the north without a word. I walked south twenty miles to the University of Iowa Hospitals and Clinics. I needed Doctor X, but he had departed for a six-month vacation. "Nurse," I screamed.

She walked into the office, where I was lying on the couch. Her dress was shorter than before. "What do you want, Nut Case?" she said.

"May I have a blanket?"

The nurse departed and returned. She dropped a bale of Irish wool beside the couch, barely missing my head. "Make it yourself, Looney Tune," she said. The door slammed louder than before.

One hundred men and women filled the therapy room of the Coralville YMCA. I stood up. "My name is Patrick," I said, "and I'm terrified of No-Name Place." The other people in the room nodded sympathetically. "The place is more frightening than a senator from Utah. I don't know what to do." I felt like crying, but I braced myself heroically.

"Have you seen Doctor X?" a 300-pound woman asked. She took a bite from her five-pound candy bar.

"Yes, once. He's on vacation for six months."

"Have you seen his nurse?" a 95-pound, six-foot man said. "She always takes my mind off my troubles." He fell off his chair. The woman put down her candy bar and helped him up.

"Yes, she tried to drop a bale of Irish wool on me," I said. "Barely missed my head."

"That's just her way of showing affection," he said. "If she doesn't like you, she drops Missouri wool on you." The woman grabbed the man by the bib of his overalls so he wouldn't fall off the chair again.

"Have you read any of our literature?" said a Jehovah's Witness. He pulled a fistful of pamphlets from his bushel basket. "They always help you forget No-Name Place."

"Haven't got around to it yet."

"Don't bother," the woman said. "They're useless."

"They're not useless," the Witness said.

"Shut up, Leroy." The woman dropped her candy bar.

"Order, order," Judge Zip said. He brushed a piece of lint from his robe.

"Drop dead, Judge." The woman let go of the overalls to pick up her candy bar, but the skinny man fell on top of it. "Fred, why don't you hold on to the chair?"

"I was thinking about the nurse."

"Remember the Sabbath and keep it holy," a Seventh Day Adventist said.

"Will that get rid of my irrational fear of No-Name Place?" I asked.

"No, but it will help me meet my quota. Have some of our literature." The Adventist reached into the bed of his pickup and pulled out some pamphlets.

"Why do you always bring your truck inside?" said the Jehovah's Witness.

"Mind your own business, Witness," the Adventist said.

"It is my business. The YMCA said no pickups inside the building."

"Order," the judge screamed. He pulled off his robe, and the skinny man set it on fire.

"This place is too dang cold," he said. He warmed his hands and rubbed them together.

"That's it. Everybody out," the manager of the Y said as she came through the door. "You can have your meetings somewhere else in the future."

Everybody walked out before the fire trucks arrived. I went to see the nurse. She barely missed me with a bale of Missouri wool.

NEVER CARNAL

ZIMBO GOT OFF THE El at Morse Avenue, walked a block south along the street facing the track, and turned in at the C'est Dommage Coffee House. The counterman watched him coming up the steps, then ran into the kitchen just as Zimbo came through the door.

I'll have to be smarter than that, thought Zimbo. He walked back to the rickety wooden door, slammed it as loudly as he could, and tiptoed into the men's john. With the lights off and the door open just a crack, he held a strategic vantage point.

The counterman peeked out of the kitchen for a moment, then ambled out to the cash register and leaned against the pastry case. He took a large comb from his back pocket and ran it through his blond hair, which stood straight up on top and was closely cropped on both sides. He put away the comb and was reaching for a toothpick when Zimbo sprang from his hiding place.

"Coffee!" Zimbo shouted as he flew through the air. He landed directly in front of the cash register. The counterman pushed himself away from the pastry case with a defeated look and reached for the coffee pot. "With cream," Zimbo said, taking some money out of his wallet. "I'd also like a bagel with cream cheese." He made this request merely to keep his spirits up. He had no expectation of ever receiving a bagel with cream cheese at the C'est Dommage Coffee House.

"Your name?" the counterman said.

"Zimbo."

"I'll call you when it's ready," he smirked, writing the name at the bottom of the check. He turned toward the kitchen, and Zimbo walked past a freezer full of melted ice cream into a long hallway.

The C'est Dommage occupied a dilapidated frame building that had once been a rooming house. The counter stood in the former parlor. Down the hallway on both sides, doors opened into small compartments, each with four miniature tables shoved into the corners. Someone had sealed off the stairway to the second floor with particle board.

In each compartment a loudspeaker tilted downward from the wall above the door. The newcomer to the C'est Dommage blithely expected to hear his order called through one of these speakers, but in five years Zimbo had never heard the slightest vibration from any of them.

He glanced into the rooms as he walked down the hall. One or two contained dejected customers, but most were empty. In the last compartment on the right, he found a fat man in a plaid shirt sitting beside a broken window. The man was pouring himself a cup of coffee from a thermos bottle.

"Hello, Dijon," Zimbo said, walking into the room. "It's a good thing you got here early and saved us a table."

The fat man pushed aside a copy of the *Daily Racing Form* and stared enviously at Zimbo's cup of coffee. "How do you do it?" he said. "I've never been able to get anything in this place."

"Gotta be fast on your feet." He sat down and took a sip. The coffee was almost warm.

The man grunted, took a puff on his cigar, and blew a dark cloud toward the ceiling. "You bring the stuff?" he said.

"Sure thing," Zimbo said. He opened a Manila envelope and tossed a small pile of typed pages onto the table.

The man put his cigar into the ashtray, picked up the pages, and began to read. Zimbo drank his coffee and looked out the window at a gutted Studebaker, which stood on four stacks of cinder blocks in a garden of broken glass.

He looked back at the fat man, who picked up his cigar and began chewing studiously. Vigo Dijon was Zimbo's literary agent. Zimbo had often wondered why a literary agent would move his lips when he read, but he thought it might be impolite to ask. He felt himself lucky to have an agent at all, especially in view of the fact that he'd never published a word and seldom read anything written after 1940.

"You sure this is what they want?" Dijon said as he put down the papers.

"Sure," Zimbo said. "They'll eat it up."

"Seems a little tame for these romance magazines. Why didn't you put more sex in it?"

"They don't want too much. I've read their tip sheets." He pulled a photocopy out of the envelope and found a sentence. "Listen to this: 'Stories should be sensual, but never carnal.'" He looked at Dijon. "They all say that—'never carnal.'"

"Okay. I got a guy to show it to. Meet us back here at nine o'clock tonight."

Dijon folded his *Racing Form*, picked up the story and the thermos bottle, and walked with Zimbo to the entrance, where a long line of customers was waiting at the cash register. The counterman was nowhere in sight.

A little man with a scruffy beard stood at the head of the line with his wallet in his hand. People in the rear milled about, looking at the menu tacked on the wall. Someone had blacked out all the items listed. So no one looked for long.

After watching Dijon drive off in his white Buick, Zimbo walked north to Greenleaf and turned toward Lake Michigan. He needed a moment of quiet reflection.

As he walked under the El, a young man in a neat business suit entered the underpass from the opposite direction. He stopped in front of Zimbo and smiled pleasantly. "Excuse me," he said, pulling a revolver from his jacket pocket. "Would you mind giving me all your money?"

"I'm afraid I don't have much," Zimbo said, reaching for his wallet. "You caught me a little short." He gave the young man his last ten dollars.

"That's all right. Have a nice day."

Zimbo continued on down the street, waited five minutes for the light at Sheridan Avenue, and walked into Loyola Park. All this happened in the 1970's, before drug gangs had seized control of this spot.

A man on a bench was describing his vacation in Miami to an old woman who was sound asleep. That's the life for me, Zimbo thought. Travel. Freedom. This romance business may be just the thing.

He walked out on the beach and reviewed the facts. His job at the Ray of Hope Greeting Card Company hadn't been so bad at first, but after two years, it had become repetitious. Every day he read three or four tubs of unsolicited iambic tetrameter. The typical submission featured end rhyme, contained two quatrains, and began with the line: "Because you mean so much to me, . . ." It was time for a change.

He walked back to the Morse Avenue El station and borrowed ten dollars from the guy who ran the newsstand. Across the street a woman was holding her purse open for the young man with the revolver. Zimbo ate dinner at the Queen Mother Delicatessen and, at exactly nine o'clock, strolled through the deserted entrance of the C'est Dommage Coffee House.

Dijon was sitting in the same place as before. "Zimbo," he said. "Here's somebody I want you to meet. This is Mr. Alpaca from *Loveburnt Magazine*. I told him all about you."

"Hello," Zimbo said.

"How do you do," Mr. Alpaca said as he got up to shake hands. He stood about seven feet tall and was as skinny as a cue stick. He wore white shoes, white socks, white pants, a white shirt, a white tie, and a white jacket. His white hat lay on the table. Zimbo assumed he had on white underwear.

"How about some coffee?" Zimbo said.

"Good idea," Dijon said. "I forgot my thermos jug."

"Coffee would be very nice," Mr. Alpaca said. He sat down and pushed his hair away from his eyes. His hair was white.

When Zimbo reached the counter, he found a plump woman in a green jogging suit drumming her fingers on the pastry case. He stepped back into the shadows of the hallway, waited a few seconds, and shouted, "Earthquake! Earthquake! Everybody out!"

The kitchen door burst open, and the counterman came sprinting through, followed by a woman with purple hair and a spotless apron. They beat the jogger to the exit by three strides.

The evacuees stood together on the sidewalk, holding their hands over their heads. Finally, the counterman looked through the door and saw Zimbo leaning against the cash register. He and the cook walked back into the building with their eyes downcast. The jogger wandered off, looking around in confusion. Zimbo got three cups of coffee and ordered six dozen bagels with cream cheese.

"You're something else, Zimbo," Dijon said as Zimbo set the coffee on the table. "I tell you, Mr. Alpaca, he's something else."

Mr. Alpaca looked up and smiled. "We've been reading your story," he said. "It's really quite good." Zimbo took a seat. "However, I'm afraid the trend today is toward more sensuousness."

"But all the tip sheets say 'never carnal.'" Zimbo said.

"I know, but all that's changing. At *Loveburnt*, we're on the cutting edge of change. We feature nothing but state-of-the-art romances."

"Listen to the man, Zimbo," Dijon said. "He knows his stuff."

"I'm listening," Zimbo said.

"Take this line, for example," Mr. Alpaca said.

"You say that 'Mitch smelled of heather and alfalfa.' I'm not sure that's the kind of image the genre calls for." He looked intently at Zimbo. His eyes were small and blue.

"I was trying to appeal to the rural crowd," Zimbo said, shifting in his seat.

"Listen, Zimbo, listen," Dijon said. He lit a cigar and filled the room with dark haze.

"Or let's consider your title," Mr. Alpaca said.

"'Love's Fury Benched' doesn't really suggest the kind of sensuousness our readers are looking for." He rested his chin on his hand and waited for a response.

"The story has a sports theme," Zimbo said. "People are very interested in athletics. I thought about calling it 'Love's Tender Fouls.'"

"Hmm," Mr. Alpaca said. Dijon flicked his ashes on the floor and examined his cigarette lighter.

"I guess I had the wrong idea," Zimbo said. He looked out the window. A family of eight was bedding down in the Studebaker.

"Well, no harm done," Mr. Alpaca said, straightening up the manuscript. "We all learn from our mistakes."

"That's right, Zimbo," Dijon said. "We all learn from our mistakes." He took the cigar out of his mouth and coughed several times.

"Right," Zimbo said.

"Besides that," Mr. Alpaca said, "there's still a lot of good material here. Why don't you let me toy around with it a bit? Then I'll get back to you."

"Sure, sure. Toy around," Dijon said, putting his cigar into the ashtray. "Right, Zimbo?"

"Right."

"Good," Mr. Alpaca said. "I'll start on it first thing tomorrow."

As they were walking to the exit, a man came out of one of the rooms and stopped them. He said he'd been waiting two hours for a bagel with cream cheese. Zimbo gave him the address of the Queen Mother Delicatessen.

The next day seemed as hopeless as ever at the Ray of Hope Greeting Card Company. Zimbo faked it all morning, had a pastrami sandwich out of a vending machine for lunch, and dragged into the afternoon. He pulled a set of poems from the brown plastic tub on the floor beside his chair, laid the pages on his desk, and began to read: "Because you mean so much to me—" The phone rang. Zimbo paper-clipped a rejection slip to the poems and tossed them into the red tub on the other side of his chair.

"Hello, Zimbo," Dijon said with his usual rasp. "I got some good news for you. *Loveburnt* bought the story. I just saw Alpaca."

"Good." Zimbo's pulse quickened slightly. "Did you tell him to use my pen name?"

"Sure. Katharine Greatwater. Just like we planned."

"Did he make many changes?"

"A few."

"Give me an example." Zimbo leaned back in his chair.

"Okay, let me look at this." Zimbo heard some papers being shuffled. "All right, here's one. He changed the location."

"How so?"

"He moved it from Indianapolis to Singapore." There was a brief pause.

"Do they like sports in Singapore?"

"I don't know, Zimbo. I don't think it matters."

"I suppose not." Zimbo leaned forward. "How much did you get?"

"What?" Dijon said.

"How much did they pay?"

"Five."

"Five what?"

"Five dollars."

"Five dollars?"

"You gotta start somewhere, Zimbo."

"I suppose." Zimbo looked at the brown tub and felt the pastrami turning over in his stomach.

"The pay'll get better."

"I hope so."

"I'll send you the money, minus seventy-five cents for my commission."

"Thanks."

"Cheer up, kid. This is your big break. They're gonna run the story issue after next."

"I can't wait."

"So long, Zimbo."

"So long." Zimbo hung up and reached into the brown tub.

Late one afternoon two months later, Zimbo stepped off the train at Morse Avenue after eight hours of metered bathos. He walked down the stairs and stopped at the newsstand. Right out front, in a neat little stack, lay the new issue of *Loveburnt Magazine.* Zimbo pulled out his wallet.

The picture on the cover showed a man and woman pawing each other in front of the Taj Mahal. Zimbo turned the page. An ad on the inside cover offered a major breakthrough in the removal of women's facial hair. Across from that was the table of contents.

When he found the name Katharine Greatwater, he saw that Mr. Alpaca had changed the name of his story.

"Love's Fury Benched" was now "Love's Furious Bulge."

He flipped through the magazine to the right page.

The text bore a slight resemblance to his original. Where he had written, "A strange sensation swept over her," the sentence now read, "A burning desire made her tremble from head to foot." What had once been "She felt his tender embrace" was now "She felt his hand between her legs." Zimbo began to get the idea.

He went outside and stopped to think. A day of iambic tetrameter had left him fatigued. He decided to take a little stroll before dinner.

He walked down to the lake and looked again at his contribution to *Loveburnt.* Maybe he should write another one. It hadn't been that hard the first time, and Dijon had said the pay would get better. He was ready to try anything to escape the Ray of Hope.

He found a telephone and slipped two dimes into the slot. "Dijon," he said, "I want to give *Loveburnt* another shot."

"That's too bad," Dijon said. "I just found out it's going out of circulation."

"What about Alpaca?"

"He's going out of circulation, too. The whole outfit was a front for a counterfeit operation. They were flooding the country with phony Hummels."

"No kidding." Zimbo leaned against the wall of the phone booth.

"Some people will try anything."

"This is a blow to literature," Zimbo said.

"You said it," Dijon said.

"What're we gonna do?" He tapped the side of the phone with his copy of *Loveburnt*.

"There's other magazines. Put something together and give me a call."

"Okay." Zimbo took a deep breath.

"And make it sensuous."

"Right."

"Set the page on fire."

"Got it."

Zimbo hung up and stepped out of the phone booth. A plane came in over the lake and descended toward O'Hare with a sullen roar. Several children were playing cops and robbers in the park. Zimbo strolled along the sidewalk, letting his mind wander.

When he reached a quiet spot near the edge of the park, he stopped and looked around. Seated on a bench off to one side, a woman with a large shopping bag was offering a shot of muscatel to a man whose brown suit was about three sizes too large. The man took a swig, then wiped his lips with the back of his hand and kissed the woman on the cheek. Zimbo felt a small bubble of excitement. That's it, he thought: "Love's Fury Bagged."

He turned and walked back to the newsstand, where he bought two ball-point pens, a writing tablet, and a bottle of aspirin. He went outside and stopped under the El to check the time.

A train came rumbling to a stop. A gust of wind sent a page from the *National Enquirer* sailing across the street. Zimbo started down the sidewalk, paused at the corner to take out his wallet for a young man with a revolver, and turned toward the C'est Dommage Coffee House.

LOOKING FOR THE ASHKENAZ DELICATESSEN

The *California Zephyr* nosed its way into the train shed and stopped three yards short of the bumping post. Zimbo waited for the herd to exit the coach. Then he descended to the lower level, grabbed his bag, and stepped onto the platform. To his right, Union Station glowed in the distance. He tipped the suitcase onto its wheels and set off for the gate.

The next morning, Zimbo emerged from the smallest room in the Palmer House, dropped to the first floor in an elevator that predated the invention of bagels, passed through the gilded lobby, and walked through the July heat to the steps leading down to the State Street subway. He'd traveled five hundred miles in order to take his breakfast at the Ashkenaz Delicatessen, and he'd acquired the appetite of a sumo wrestler who'd lost his cafeteria card.

The Howard Street train carried Zimbo under the Chicago River and up into the sunlight of the elevated track that led to Roger's Park. The Ashkenaz Delicatessen waited thirty minutes to the north. It seemed that he'd left it only a week ago, but that's how everything now seemed.

Zimbo climbed off the train at Morse Avenue and looked down the street toward the west. Something was missing. The Jewel store was missing. The plumbing-supply store had disappeared. The people had vanished. Where was everybody? Zimbo went down the steps from the elevated platform and turned right toward the Ashkenaz Delicatessen. A short walk took him to the familiar address, where he found the saddest place in Chicago, a lot so vacant that it matched the entire city council. "Where's the delicatessen?" Zimbo said to a passing drunk.

"Up there," the man said, motioning toward the north or toward Lake Michigan. His movements lacked the grace of a successful tour guide. "I don't have any money."

Zimbo gave the man two dollars. "Get something to eat," he said.

"Sure," the man said. "Something to eat."

Zimbo wandered around until he found an open-air telephone booth, the kind that isn't really a booth at all, the kind that invites bandits to take everything you have and shoot you for not having the exact change. The booth displayed drug-gang graffiti, empty Thunderbird bottles, and a severed cord where the receiver should have been. Zimbo returned to the El and caught a train back to the Loop, where he returned to his lonely garret in the Palmer House. He would have to find a friend or relative. Only one friend or relative came to mind. He picked up the telephone and punched in a number. "Hello, Connie," he said. "This is Zimbo."

Silence.

"You know," he said, "your husband."

"Oh, you." She said "you" as if the word was a foot fungus.

"Yes me. Aren't you glad to hear my voice?"

"No. Where are you?"

"The Palmer House. I've booked the presidential suite for the year."

"That's unfortunate. I thought you'd fallen in love with Omaha."

"The mystic chords have called me home."

"What do you want from me? I don't have any money."

"I'm looking for the Ashkenaz Delicatessen. I need the best lox this side of Paradise."

"It's on Morse Avenue. Why'd you call me?"

"It's gone. Something severed the mystic chords. There's nothing there but a vacant lot."

"I didn't hear about this. How do you know?"

"The empirical method, Connie. I went up for a look. It's gone, absent, disappeared, missing and assumed dead. Doesn't this trouble you?"

"It troubles me, but you trouble me more."

"Can't you ask somebody from the old home place? You must have at least one friend north of the Cook County Jail."

"All right, all right, I'll call somebody." She hung up.

The next morning, after lengthy negotiations, Zimbo arrived at the elevated platform at Howard Street, where he found Connie and the Skokie Swift waiting. Connie stared at him. Her eyes were as dark as Franz Kafka's.

At 10:15 AM, Connie boarded the first car, and Zimbo boarded the second, which was also the last. At 10:19 AM, the train pulled away from the platform and turned westward with the course of empire, the white man's burden, and the Mormon Tabernacle Choir.

At this point, the train descended to a level that was neither elevated nor subterranean. Instead, the track dropped into a declivity reminiscent of the Natchez Trace, that homeward route followed by sturdy flatboat men from Natchez to Nashville in the antebellum period. On both sides of the trench, trees blocked the sky.

Zimbo looked around the car but saw no sturdy flatboat men. He saw a middle-aged man and woman dressed in shorts and golf shirts. He saw a teen-aged boy and a teen-aged girl who gave every indication that sex on the Swift would please them more than anything that ever happened between Natchez and Nashville. At 10:27, after a 90-degree turn to the north, the Skokie Swift came to a stop at the end of the line, Skokie, Illinois.

The temperature had risen to 98 degrees in the shade, but there was no shade between the end of the line and the sign atop the Skokie Delicatessen, which stood half a block away. While maintaining a distance of thirty yards, Zimbo followed Connie toward the sign.

By the time he walked through the door, thirty yards behind Connie, the manager had given her samples of corned beef, pastrami, salami, lox novo, and lox non-novo. Tubs of cream cheese stood on all sides. The manager, a woman older than Zimbo, required a final judgement. "You're right," Connie said. "The pastrami is good, but the corned beef is excellent."

Zimbo stopped five yards away. "Yes?" the manager said.

"He's my husband," Connie said. "Ignore him. I'll take five pounds of corned beef. Zimbo, give her the money."

Zimbo found his wallet and pulled out a pile of tens. "This is gonna finish me off," he said.

"Just pay it."

Zimbo walked over to the cash register, which rang and whirled like a slot machine. "Here's your change," said the clerk.

Zimbo took the dime and held it up to the light. "Looks okay," he said. "Do you know where the Ashkenaz Delicatessen is?" he said to the manager.

"The Ashkenaz Delicatessen?" she said. "What era was that?"

"Precambrian."

"Where you been?"

"Away on business."

"Un-huh."

"Someone told us it moved to Skokie."

"No. It moved downtown, but I don't think it lasted."

"This is a tragedy."

"You'll survive. Try the corned beef."

Zimbo returned to the Loop one train behind Connie. He had work to do, but didn't know what. He walked into the lobby of the Palmer House and stopped in the center to ponder the mystery of the Ashkenaz

Delicatessen. Five minutes later, a tall blue-suited man reeking of officialdom walked over and said, "May I help you, sir?"

"What?"

"May I help you?"

"Who are you?"

"Palmer House security."

"You?"

"Yes, sir."

"Where's the Ashkenaz Delicatessen?"

The man gave this less than a moment of thought. "I don't recall that place. Would you like to look in the Chicago yellow pages?"

Serotonin flooded Zimbo's brain. His synapses began firing like AK-47s. "Yes," he said. "Yes."

"Sir, could I see your room key." Zimbo pulled the key from his pocket and made it go jingle-jangle. "This way, sir."

Zimbo followed the hotel cop into a small room off the lobby. "Here we are, sir, the yellow pages. Why don't you sit at my desk and look up the delicatessen. I'll be in the lobby if you need me. Take your time."

Zimbo sat down and flipped to section A. He found "Ashkenazim this" and "Ashkenazim that" before he finally found the Ashkenaz Delicatessen and Internet Café on East Cedar Street. He also looked up the Sephardic Delicatessen, but section S of the yellow pages suggested that it didn't exist.

He picked up the phone and dialed the number on East Cedar. "Buzz, buzz, buzz, etc."

"This is the Ashkenaz Delicatessen and Internet Café. Please leave a message, and we'll—"

Zimbo hung up, waited two minutes, and dialed again. The phone was still busy. Zimbo gave up and called Connie's cell phone.

"Hello." Zimbo heard the sound of street traffic in Oak Park.

"I found something called the Ashkenaz Delicatessen and Internet Café on East Cedar Street."

"Internet Café?"

"Yes."

"Zimbo, why are you such an imbecile?"

"Bad toilet training. This might be the place. Don't you want to check it out?"

Silence for a few seconds. "Oh, all right."

"I'll meet you at Clark and Division at ten in the morning."

"Do you mean in the subway with the other rodents or up in the sunlight?"

"In the sunlight. If we walk down Division and turn right on State, we can slip past the toxic vapors of Rush Street."

"Okay," Connie said. "Be on time."

"Will do," Zimbo said.

Connie hung up, and Zimbo went up to his room. He forgot to say good-bye to Palmer House security.

At 10:01 AM, Zimbo popped out of the subway. Connie looked at her watch. "You're a minute late."

"Sorry."

"Let's go. Stay thirty yards behind me."

"Why do you always want me to stay thirty yards behind? Why not ten yards, or five?"

"I don't want anyone to think I'm with you. It would destroy my reputation."

"You used to walk with me. This could harm my self-esteem."

"All right, ten yards. Let's go."

Zimbo followed Connie down Division, turned right on State, and took a sharp left at Cedar, thereby barely inhaling the stench of Rush Street. By the time he entered the Ashkenaz Delicatessen and Internet Café, Connie had engaged the attention of a short, rotund, hairy male. "If this isn't the Ashkenaz Delicatessen that used to be on Morse Avenue," Connie said, "why do you call it the Ashkenaz Delicatessen?"

"You forgot the part about the Internet Café," the man said. His hairiness was uniformly dark.

"What difference does that make?" Connie was waving her arms as she talked. "What people remember is the Ashkenaz Delicatessen part."

"No they don't."

"Yes they do."

Zimbo feared violence, from Connie. "Could I have a bagel with cream cheese novo and lox non-novo?" he said to initiate a cooling-off period.

"We don't have novo anything," the man said. His face had turned red beneath his dark stubble.

"Don't yell at my husband," Connie said.

"That's right," Zimbo said. "Don't yell at her husband." He stepped behind her.

"You still haven't said why you used the name Ashkenaz Delicatessen," Connie said.

"Right," Zimbo said.

The man ignored Zimbo, who was now out of sight, out of mind. "Do you have any idea how many Ashkenaz Delicatessens there are in this country? Dozens, hundreds, thousands."

"I don't believe it," Connie said.

"Are you calling me a liar?" the man shouted.

"Yes," Connie shouted.

Ninety minutes later, after the police had left in their blue and white patrol cars, Connie and Zimbo walked two blocks north on State Street and turned left on Division. Behind them, Lake Michigan lapped at the shore while a stream of traffic rolled along Lake Shore Drive. Out of sight to the north, the hardwood trees in Lincoln Park wilted in the heat. At State and Division, people in business clothes hurried to lunch.

"I guess it's hopeless," Zimbo said.

"What?" Connie said.

"We'll never find the Ashkenaz Delicatessen because it no longer exists."

"So it seems."

A beer truck approached from the west, filled the air with exhaust fumes, and turned toward Rush Street.

"I'll just check out of the hotel and go back to Omaha."

"Try not to get drunk on the train."

They walked two blocks to the steps that led down to the subway. "Which way you going?" Zimbo said.

"I think I'll go up to Evanston to see my sister," Connie said.

"Okay, I'll see you later."

"Sure."

"Connie."

"Yes?" She looked at him with less annoyance than usual.

"Thanks for the walk."

NEW ZEALAND NEW

JAMES NOLAND WALKED DOWN Derby Street, genuflected internally at the gray-stucco walls of St. Brigid's Church, continued on to Parnell Street, and turned in at the sidewalk to his house. But instead of going through the front door, he walked around to the back to inspect his new deck. Was he, he wondered, the only American in New Zealand stupid enough to pay $12,000 for a large deck attached to a small house?

Noland had wanted only a set of stairs to the back door. "But I want a deck," Colette had said. "Everybody in Feilding has one. I want to have my friends over, and I don't want them piled up in the lounge."

Lounge, scrounge, Noland said to himself. Let them pile up on their own $12,000 decks.

"Hello, Jim," Colette shouted from the lounge as Noland went through the back door.

"Hello, Love," Noland said. "I survived another day of service to humanity."

Colette swept into the kitchen like an English battleship poised to unload a barrage at the *Bismarck*. "Did you get the wine?"

"Wine?"

"Yes, wine. I told you Susan and Robert were coming to dinner tonight."

"Dinner tonight?"

"Yes, tonight. Stop echoing everything I say."

"Echoing?"

Colette giggled. "Stop that, you idiot."

"Sorry."

"I forgive you."

Noland aimed his twenty-year-old Saab down Derby Street, turned right on Kimbolton Road, and drove straight toward the clock tower and the roundabout where you had to go left to get right.

"Sometimes I regret getting married," he said to the Saab. "It's too expensive." The Saab coughed and went left to get right.

Noland turned into the parking lot at Feilding Foods, parked the car, and turned off the ignition. The Saab coughed and died. "I could get a divorce if I weren't a Catholic," Noland said aloud as he climbed out. A young woman looked at Noland and quickly got into her car. "I don't even believe in God," he said. Noland leaned against the door of the Saab. "I guess I believe sometimes." The woman locked her car doors. Colette isn't so bad when she isn't borrowing money." The woman started her car and backed into a shopping cart. "And she laughs at most of my jokes."

Noland walked into the store and retrieved a case of Sentura Sauvignon Blanc. "God bless Argentina," he said to the cashier.

Noland climbed the ladder to the roof of the house. "You're going to kill yourself," Colette said.

"There are times when a corps commander's life doesn't count," Noland said.

"Who said that?"

"A Union general supposedly said it at the Battle of Gettysburg. He should've taken cover, but he rode his horse up and down the line of battle to give his men courage."

"This isn't the Battle of Gettysburg."

"Yes it is. The opossums are trying to destroy our perfect union." He carried the chicken wire, the hammer, and the staples up the sloping metal roof to the chimney. He peered inside to look for opossums. Dark as a forgotten coal mine. "Here we go," he said.

He put the chicken wire over the top of the chimney and bent it down on all four sides. Then he took a staple out of the bag and started to drive it into the mortar to hold the wire in place. The staple bent, fell to the roof, and slid down into the gutter. "I told you it wouldn't work," Colette said.

"That's right," Noland said. "That's what you told me."

"And I was right."

"And you were right."

"Let Bill do it."

Noland laid the hammer across the chimney to keep the wire in place. "Okay, give him a call."

Colette drove south toward Wellington as the Saab filled the air with a deadly black haze. Noland looked over at her profile. Her slender nose ran straight from top to tip and formed a gentle angle. The eyelids of her left eye opened to display the entire blue iris. The natural curls of her blond hair covered her ear and stopped at her shoulder. "We should've traded cars years ago," she said.

"We're not rich," Noland said. "I don't like going into debt."

"If you made more money, you wouldn't mind."

"I'm sorry I don't make more money. I'll quit teaching and open a bank when we get back to Feilding."

"I wasn't joking."

Noland looked out the window on his left. Sheep covered the green hills. The grass was always green in New Zealand, just as in Ireland. "I know you weren't," he said.

"If jokes were money, we'd be rich."

Noland looked back at Colette. "If we could've had children, would you be happier," he said.

Colette pondered for fifty meters. "Yes," she said.

"Would you like to move back to America?"

"No."

Colette did the talking at Wellington Wheels. Noland knew that she had a better head for business. He felt the tread on the tires, listened to the engine, turned all the lights on and off, and tried to decode the information on the paper attached to the window of the Camry. "Is this a New Zealand new?" Colette said.

"Yes it is, Colette," the salesman said. "Came here straight from the factory. One-owner car. Has a new warrant of fitness, Colette."

Noland stared at the salesman, a short, stocky fellow who spoke faster than seemed possible.

"Do you have a service history?"

"Yes, Colette. The previous owner kept complete records. I can show them to you, Colette."

Noland wondered if the salesman would remember his name. "How many previous owners did you say there were?" he said.

"Just one, Jim. Just one."

Colette started to giggle, but suppressed it. "Do you offer a warranty?" she asked.

"Yes, Colette. One year, two year, three year, Colette."

"One year, two year, three year," Noland repeated.

Colette repressed another giggle. "You're asking too much for a ten-year-old Camry with one hundred fifty thousand K on it," she said. "Would you take six thousand for it?"

A painful expression contorted the salesman's face. "I can't go that low, Colette."

"Let me drive it, and we'll talk some more," she said.

Colette drove the car to an on ramp. At 5:15 PM, traffic was heavy on the motorway. Colette hit the gas pedal, and the Camry took off like a thoroughbred leaving the starting gate in New South Wales.

"Nice piece of horseflesh," Noland said.

"Let's find a hill," Colette said. She exited the motorway and found a country road with a steep hill. She started up the hill at thirty kilometers per hour, goosed the engine, and the car quickly hit one hundred and ten.

"Better slow down," Noland said. "The sheep will give you a ticket."

"I want this car," Colette said. She slowed down, found a place to turn around, and headed back toward Wellington. "Please don't make me laugh when I'm talking to the salesman."

"Won't say a thing, Colette. Won't make a sound, Colette."

"How'd it go, Colette?" the salesman said. "In great condition, isn't it, Colette?"

"This car lacks power," Colette said. "It's not worth what you're asking. I'll give you six thousand, plus the Saab as a trade-in. That's as high as I'll go. You can take it or let the car sit here and rust." Noland looked at Colette with admiration and didn't say a thing.

"I'll have to talk to the owner, Colette." The salesman walked into the office and emerged a few minutes later. "I can let you have it for six thousand five hundred, plus the Saab, Colette."

"I told you six thousand was as high as I'd go," Colette said.

The salesman let his shoulders drop. "You can have it," he said. He forgot to say "Colette."

Noland stepped onto the $12,000 deck and surveyed Colette's garden: calla lilies, hibiscuses, roses of many colors, petunias, gardenias, rhododendrons, bromeliads, begonias, clematises, fuchsias of many varieties, peach trees, apple trees, lemon trees, grapefruit trees, a grape arbor, and many other plants and trees that Noland couldn't name or spell.

But there in the midst of it all, Noland saw something that made him realize why Colette had really wanted the deck. On three strong pieces of wire, all emerging from where she had pushed the ends into the ground, she had threaded small white conch shells in a way that made them look like delphiniums.

Colette had said she didn't want her friends piled up in the lounge. What she hadn't said was that she did want them piled up on the deck, where they could see her garden and its magic delphiniums. How clever she was. For a moment, Noland's thoughts verged on sentimentality, until he remembered the $12,000.

Colette and Noland stood in St. Brigid's Church as Father Moore began the Lord's Prayer. Noland started to say, "Forgive us our trespasses" instead of "Forgive us our sins," but Colette gave him a sharp elbow in the ribs. Noland always believed in God while at Mass. At other times, his faith often suffered. After the prayer, he said, "Peace be with you," first to Colette, then to the other people around him, and he meant it every time.

After the alter servers had helped Father Moore prepare for the Eucharist, he raised the wafer with both hands. "This is the Lamb of God," he said, "who takes away the sins of the world." Noland saw the wafer, and he believed, just as he had as a child in the little country church in Iowa. He saw it all again—the wafer, the white church, the corn rows in the field beyond the graveyard, and the dust rising from the gravel road.

That church was closed and shuttered now, but Noland saw it as it once had been: the slanted sunlight that shone from the east, his parents and sister beside him, the altar, the two candles, the wafer that Father Rossi raised high for the small gathering.

And when Mass had ended, Noland followed Colette outside, where he found that his vision of the little church in Iowa had left him, just as it always did, just as everything did. He held Colette's hand as they walked down the sidewalk. Then he climbed into the white Camry, and Colette drove them home.

DARK MATTER

SPRING COMES TO THE Middle West. Season of warm breezes and nitrate alerts. The water in the Des Moines River is as deadly as tax law.

At the Iowa Correspondence Institute on the bank of the river, Vice-President Harold Tiegler-Smith motions to David Himmel to sit down. "Himmel," he says, "the president is nervous about low enrollments. We need a new course, a moneymaker."

Himmel ponders. His hair is blond, his eyes blue. He has a gap between his two front teeth. "T.S.," he says, "I have just the thing."

"Let's hear it." Tiegler-Smith leans forward. His small gray eyes lock on Himmel's face.

"Dark matter."

"What?"

"Dark matter. I read an article about it. It's out in space. Everywhere. Between the stars, between the galaxies, that's where you'll find it. Biggest thing in the universe."

"What's it made of? What's it look like?"

"Don't know, T.S. No one's ever seen it. Too dark."

"What will it do for us?"

"Raise enrollments. Increase revenue. Make the president happy as a squirrel."

"Does Minnesota have it?"

"Nope. It's all ours."

Tiegler-Smith leans back in his leather chair. "So was the History of Disco."

༶

Himmel returns to his cubicle and compiles a list of materials for Introduction to Dark Matter: textbooks, telescope, tripod, folding chair, astronomical charts, insect repellent, rain slicker. Correction: delete rain slicker; add flashlight. Total cost: $300. Charge to student: $600. Tuition: $400. Tuition plus materials: $1000. Subtract $300 in costs: $700 profit per student. Estimated enrollment for first year: 1000. Profit for year: $700,000. Investment in inventory for year: $300,000.

Himmel summarizes the content of Introduction to Dark Matter:

1. History of astronomy. Ptolemy to present. Causes. Effects.

2. Discovery of dark matter. Who did it? Where? How? Why?

3. Dark matter. What is it? Where is it? How big is it? Cannot see it. Cannot see through it. Out in space. Between other things.

4. Future of dark matter. Trends. Goals. Costs.

Himmel plans his publicity campaign. Press release to *USA Today* and *Grit*. Talk shows. Billboards. Testimonials. Barn signs. Emphasize income potential. Benefits of correspondence study: no driving, no parking, no need to get dressed, no need to stay awake.

Himmel reports to Tiegler-Smith.

"Himmel," Tiegler-Smith says. "We'll never get that many students."

"Yes we will. Unless . . ."

"Unless what?"

"Unless Minnesota gets them first."

Himmel spends the rest of the day preparing the course. His brain works like a dynamo. He compiles reading assignments, writing assignments, and viewing assignments. He writes summaries, study questions, and examinations.

Afternoon heads toward evening. Himmel works faster. The phone rings. He unplugs it. Someone walks in. Himmel ignores him/her. Phones ring in other cubicles. Himmel rips up his handkerchief and stuffs his ears. He ignores backache, writer's cramp, dyspepsia, and hair loss. At six o'clock he calls his wife and says he'll be late. She promises to kiss Jimmy, Annie, Bobby, etc., for him. He finishes at midnight.

The first student to enroll is Roberta Flora. She lives in western Nebraska, where, she writes, "The sky fills the nights like nowhere else." A segment from one of her essays:

> Does dark matter cause the light from distant galaxies to bend? Does it obscure the light from other galaxies, causing them to appear only as faint blue spots when seen through powerful telescopes? Do tiny particles of dark matter constantly pass through our bodies, affecting us in unknown and incalculable ways? Do these particles collect in our eyes and fall like black snow through our vision? Does the universe, in fact, consist almost entirely of dark matter? Or is all this a sad metaphor for the dark matter of the soul?

Dear Ms. Flora:
Your essay asks many questions. But not the right ones. Think about the important questions: How do you measure dark matter? How much exists? What does it weigh? Where do you find it? What is it worth?
Think size. Think volume.
Sincerely,
David Himmel

Time passes.

The phone rings. "Himmel?"
"Yes."
"I need the figures for Introduction to Dark Matter by nine o'clock tomorrow morning. I have to see the president. Don't be late."
Himmel looks at his watch. It's already four in the afternoon. He bends over his desk. Blue light from fluorescent bulbs fills the cubicle.

Phones ring. A shredder chews. Computers beep. Copy machines churn. A fly buzzes. Himmel tries to concentrate. What can he say? What can he do?

At ten o'clock his phone rings. His wife says, "Why don't you come home? You're never home. You've been this way ever since you heard about dark matter. I'm sick of it. I'm sick of dark matter!"

She hangs up and Himmel looks at his report. Enrollments to date: one. Total revenue to date: $1000. Total profit to date: $700. Amount remaining in inventory: $299,700.

Dear Mr. Himmel:

I am writing to express my reservations about the course. Do we really need to catalog and describe dark matter? Does it matter what shape it is? Must we calculate its worth? Is it the mere size or amount of it that makes it important? Or does dark matter have a value that cannot be measured or even named?

Sincerely,

Roberta Flora

Himmel drafts a profile of the typical student in Introduction to Dark Matter:

Age: 32.

Sex: female.

Occupation: farm wife.

Marital status: married.

Children: 2.

Address: western Nebraska.

Interests: dark matter.

DARK MATTER
FINAL EXAMINATION

Directions: Answer all three questions.

Time limit: Two hours.

1. Discuss dark matter. What is it? Where is it? What size is it? What is it made of? Who discovered it? How? Can we see it? If so, what does it look like? If not, how do we know it's there?

2. Compare and contrast dark matter and black holes. Are they the same thing? If so, why two names? If not, how do they differ? Are they found in the same places? Made of the same materials? Why dark? Why black?

3. Discuss the political implications of dark matter.

EXAM BOOKLET

NAME: Roberta Flora
COURSE: Dark Matter

I am unable to complete the examination. Dark matter cannot be located, analyzed, or explained. It exists in a universe we can sense, but never comprehend. We cannot describe dark matter, yet our world would be empty without it. How, then, can I answer your questions? And if I cannot, what is the purpose of the course? And what is the value of the Iowa Correspondence Institute?

Dear Ms. Flora:

I understand now. You were right all along. Only you took the course because only you saw the possibilities. This is why only you could explain its failure. I understand this now. But now it may be too late. The course is written, the warehouse full, the money spent. I fear for the future of dark matter.

Sincerely,

David Himmel

Later, following his dismissal from the Iowa Correspondence Institute, Harold Tiegler-Smith left Des Moines for Minneapolis, where he became vice-president at the Minnesota Correspondence Institute.

After refusing to complete the final examination for Introduction to Dark Matter, Roberta Flora abandoned her husband and children and took a job at an all-night diner in Omaha. She subsequently resigned and moved away without leaving a forwarding address.

While on a family vacation in the Black Hills of South Dakota, David Himmel walked out of his motel room in the dark of night and disappeared into the Pine Ridge Indian Reservation. He left a note stating his intention to "find Sitting Bull's ghost."

Several months later Patrick Noland, a former colleague, spotted Himmel coming out of an Art Deco movie theater in St. Paul after a showing of the *film noir* classic *D.O.A.* He was accompanied by a woman matching the description of Roberta Flora. They walked down the street and turned into an alley. Noland tried to catch up, but when he reached the alley, he couldn't see a thing. Too dark.

No one has seen them since.

FLIPPERS

Part i

"Piss on your hanging desk tops," Margaret said.

"What?" Boxwell said.

"Piss on them. I want conventional desks with four legs."

"Let's not be rude," Nick said. "Mr. Boxwell is just giving us the possibilities." He scratched his mustache.

"He is, is he? Well let me give you something." Her violet eyes narrowed and held him with a motionless stare. "I don't want you putting my people in those cubicles like rats in a Skinner box."

"Action offices," Boxwell said. He gave her a tolerant smile.

"What?" Margaret said.

"They're called action offices, not cubicles."

"I don't care what they're called. I don't want them."

"They have lots of advantages."

"Like what?"

"They'll help you achieve maximum energy distribution."

"This isn't a power plant."

"I know, but we're going to help you become more efficient. That's what our open-office systems do. They help you become more efficient."

"Not if everything gets stolen. How can we lock up the exams if we don't have doors?"

"Flippers."

"Flippers?"

"That's right. Flippers." He showed her a photograph. "See these little panels? They have shelves behind them. You flip them up to open them and flip them down to lock them. That's why they're called flippers."

"See?" Nick said. "They thought of everything." He brushed some dandruff off the shoulder of his blue suit.

"Uh-huh," Margaret said. "Did they think about the noise—phones ringing, people talking? How can anyone work in a place like that?"

"Sound-absorbing materials," Boxwell said.

"Forgive me," Margaret said. "I should've known."

There was a period of silence.

"Marv," Nick said, "why don't you tell her the antidote you told me yesterday."

"What?" Boxwell said.

"You know. The antidote. The story about the computer company."

"Oh yes." He smiled again. "Well, Margaret, we installed one of our efficient open-office systems for a leading computer company last year, and they improved their productivity by ten percent."

"Ten percent of their people must've quit."

"I don't know about that. They didn't say."

More silence.

"Just think about it," Nick said. "You'll see the advantages." He scratched his head, and a new shower of dandruff fell on his jacket.

"That's right," Boxwell said. "It's a great system. You'll love the earth-tone colors."

"Earth-tone colors?" Margaret said.

"You bet. Very ecological."

Margaret rested her forehead on the palm of her hand and closed her eyes.

PART 2

"I hate to have to tell you this," Cindy said, "but I'm leaving."

"You mean for good?" Margaret said.

"Yes." Her eyes turned toward the floor.

"I'm sorry to hear that."

"I feel guilty, after you were nice enough to hire me and everything." She looked back at Margaret.

"That's all right. You don't have to feel guilty."

"It's just that now that I know what it's like to work in a place like this, I don't think I want to stay here the rest of my life."

"I know what you mean." Margaret pushed a strand of hair up off her forehead. Her hair was a blend of blonde and gray.

"I'm going back to grad school. I think I can stick it out this time."

"I'm sure you can. I envy you."

"I never expected to hear you say that. I've always envied you."

Margaret didn't reply.

"Anyway," Cindy said, "I'm sorry."

"It'll be hard to replace you," Margaret said, "but you have to do what's best for you. We'll get along all right."

Cindy hesitated a moment. "I wonder if all jobs are like this. It all seems so meaningless."

"That's really the problem here, isn't it? It's meaningless." She looked at the papers on her desk. "Sooner or later you realize it's all a big joke and there's nothing you can do about it."

"There's something I can do," Cindy said.

PART 3

Margaret walked to the center of the maze and sat down on a granite bench. The maze stood on the grounds of the old Barker estate, directly across the street from the building Margaret worked in. Thaddeus Barker had made his fortune in the nineteenth century, selling stock in railroads that never got built. Forty years after Barker's death, his grandson gave the estate to the city, which subsequently turned the mansion into an art museum surrounded by a twenty-acre park.

Margaret had found this spot ten years before, her second day on the job. After eating her yogurt and banana, she'd suddenly realized she had no idea how to get out of the labyrinth of tall bushes. A little, dark-eyed girl had shown her the way.

Ever since that afternoon, she'd been afraid she might get lost again. Even now, as she spread her lunch out beside her, she felt a small tremor of fear.

She knew this was silly—the maze wasn't that difficult—but she couldn't help it.

She ate her cheese and her carrot sticks, then shared her bread with a solitary pigeon. A breeze found its way into the labyrinth, and the sound of traffic came from the street. Margaret ate her apple, then leaned back with her face toward the sun. The insides of her eyelids turned the color of fire.

Part 4

Margaret switched on the lights and sat down at her desk. A copy of *Words into Type* lay to one side, next to a desk calendar filled with scribbled reminders. She picked up a new set of questions and began to read:

1. At one point in Franz Kafka's story "The Metamorphosis," Gregor crawls onto a picture frame. What does this symbolize?

A. Moses.

B. Mohammed.

C. Buddha.

D. Jesus.

Margaret put the questions down, stood up, and walked to the window. Ten stories below, traffic was heavy on Carver Boulevard. At the intersection with Hancock Street, the stoplights had quit working, and a policeman was trying to sort out a tangle of cars and trucks.

The phone rang.

"You want us to run this real-estate test on the web press, don't you?" a male voice said.

"Yes," Margaret said.

"The order said sheet-fed, but I didn't think that was right."

"No. Run it on the web."

She hung up and read the next question:

2. The work of Jorge Luis Borges could best be described as_____.

A. interior

B. exterior

C. anterior

D. posterior

She stood up, went out to the water fountain, and walked back into the office without getting a drink. A woman came in and left a stack of illustrations on her desk.

Margaret picked up the illustrations and set them back down. She picked up some questions and set them back down. She reached for the phone.

"How do the apple trees look?" she said.

"They look all right," her sister said. "We just started picking."

"Do you have enough help?"

"I never have enough help."

"How's Mom?"

"Same as always."

"Tell her hello. I'll call you tonight."

Margaret put the phone down and looked at another question.

3. In Greek mythology, how did Daedalus escape from the Labyrinth?

A. By land.

B. By sea.

C. By air.

D. He didn't escape.

PART 5

Stacks of paper littered Margaret's desk. She was trying to concentrate on a set of questions when Nick walked into the office without knocking. "Excuse me, Margaret," he said, "but I've been meaning to talk to you."

She looked at him without answering. He sat down and brushed some dandruff from his sleeve.

"You know," he said, "you and your people deserve a lot of credit. You've all done a quality job."

Margaret closed her eyes and opened them slowly.

"What I like the most about your operation," he went on, "is the way you always lend a hand when something comes up."

"What's come up this time?" Margaret said.

"Nothing more than what we talked about this morning. Just this new office configuration."

"I don't like your new office configuration."

"I know, but we all have to make sacrifices."

"Why?"

"We have to keep our expenses down. Costs keep going up, so we have to find ways to operate more efficiently. It's the same here as it is at home. Everyone's trying to save money. My wife has even started buying genetic toilet paper."

Margaret felt the urge to smash something against the wall. "The trouble with you," she said, leaning forward, "is that you're always trying to operate more efficiently, and all you ever do is foul things up."

"I'm just doing my job."

"I know. That's the problem. *Stop* doing your job. Leave things alone."

"Oh, I can't do that. We're striving for excellence."

Margaret fell back in the chair.

"Anyway," Nick said, "I need your help with this project."

"What do you mean?"

"We need to cooperate with Marv. He's here to design the best possible office environment."

"He's here to design the best possible sales."

"Well, you can't blame him for that, can you?"

"Why not?"

"Money's the name of the game. Everyone knows that. That's what we're all here for."

Margaret hesitated a moment. "You're right," she said. "That is what we're all here for."

Part 6

Margaret was staring at the piles of paper on her desk, trying to decide which one to pick up, when a knock sounded at the door. Boxwell popped his head in and displayed his teeth. "Hello again," he said.

"Hello, Boxhead," Margaret said.

"Well," he said as he walked in.

"Well what?"

"Boxwell. My name's Boxwell, not Boxhead."

"Okay, Boxhead, I stand corrected. What do you want?"

Boxwell looked confused, but recovered quickly. "May I sit down?" he said, showing his teeth again.

"Go ahead." She pointed at a chair.

He sat down and took a notebook out of his briefcase. "I need to chat with you a bit to make sure we get the right configuration for your personnel."

Margaret shuddered.

Boxwell took a ball-point pen out of his shirt pocket, aimed it at the notebook, and looked up at Margaret. "The first thing I need to ask," he said, "is how many employees do you have?"

"Eight white rats and a gerbil," Margaret said.

"I see. Does that mean nine?"

Margaret nodded.

"Plus you, right?" Boxwell said.

She nodded again.

"So we need ten action offices and a conference module," Boxwell said, writing something in the notebook.

Margaret shuddered again.

Boxwell looked up from the notebook. "How many flippers do you want in each office?"

"Nine hundred and fifty."

"There's only room for two in each action office." He waited, but she didn't respond. "I'll put you down for two per office." He wrote something else.

"You'd probably like an extra work surface in each office, wouldn't you?" he said. "In addition to your hanging desk tops."

"Uh-huh."

"How many square feet would you like?"

"Twenty-five thousand."

"There's only room for sixteen per office." He looked at her, but she didn't reply. "I'll put you down for sixteen."

He finished writing, closed the notebook, and looked up again. "Well," he said, "that's all I need for now. Do you have any questions?"

"Who's buried in Grant's Tomb?"

"What?"

"Who's buried in Grant's Tomb? You asked me if I had any questions."

"I don't know." He looked worried.

"Haven't you read Marx?"

"Who?"

"Groucho Marx, the famous economic theorist and quiz-show host."

"I don't think so," he said. "I'll have to look him up."

PART 7

Across the river the five o'clock whistle sounded at the power plant, and all over town men and women headed for home. They traveled down roads that connected with other roads that connected with still others in a labyrinth that reached from Duluth to Del Rio, from Boston to Bakersfield.

Margaret stood at the window, watching the rush-hour traffic on Carver Boulevard. In the hall behind her, the members of her staff were leaving for the day. The elevator doors opened and closed, and silence filled the tenth floor.

A few minutes later the elevator doors opened again, and Margaret heard someone walking down the hall to her office.

"Hello, Margaret," Nick said. "I just wanted to tell you that Marv said he had a nice chat with you."

Margaret continued to stare out the window. "What was nice about it?" she said.

"He said he got all the information he needed."

"Good for him. Now maybe he'll drop dead."

There was a lengthy pause.

"I know how you feel about this, Margaret, but someday you'll see the advantages. Remember, it's always darkest at dawn."

Margaret's body trembled violently.

"Well, good night," Nick said. "See you tomorrow."

He went off down the hall, and Margaret stayed at the window, looking down at the traffic. One car had run into another, and both drivers were out in the street, surveying the damage. The drivers behind them were using their horns.

Margaret opened the window as far as she could, then walked over to her desk. Stacks of paper covered the entire surface. She picked up a small pile and went back to the window.

Down in the street, the two drivers involved in the accident were still peering at their cars. The sound of horns had reached a crescendo. Margaret drew a deep breath and exhaled like a woman reprieved.

One by one, she started dropping the papers out the window. Some of the people on the ground saw her and pointed up. Then others saw her, and the sound of horns began to subside.

Margaret began dropping the papers faster, and the people started to cheer. She began dropping three or four at a time, and they cheered even louder. All traffic came to a stop.

When the stack of paper was gone, Margaret went back to the desk for a bigger one. She could see that this was going to take a while. She walked to the window and leaned on the sill. The breeze felt cool on her face.

Most of the people were out of their cars by now. Pedestrians stood on the sidewalks. Everyone was watching Margaret. She braced herself and threw the entire stack out the window as hard as she could.

Down below, the crowd sent up its loudest cheer yet. The papers held together for a moment, then fell apart in the breeze and drifted down on Carver Boulevard. Like dandruff on a man's suit. Like apple blossoms in May.

THE VOICE OF THE CUBS

Timothy Billows found a room for rent in Wanganui, less than two blocks from the telephone exchange. Then he walked through the rain to the exchange office. "Will this room give me high-speed internet, broadband, and uninterrupted service?" he said to the telephone man.

"Yes, maybe, and no," the man said. He was tall and knobby, and looked like Ichabod Crane.

"Can you flip the switch today?"

"No."

Tim gave him fifty dollars. "Can you flip the switch today?"

"Yes."

"This is important."

"Why?"

"I'm going to become the voice of the Cubs."

The man stared at him for a moment. "Have a nice day," he said.

Tim walked around Wanganui in the rain. Thirty minutes later, he found the landlord at the off-track betting shop. "I'll take the room," Tim said.

"It's four hundred dollars a month, plus a hundred more if you want me to hook up the sink and toilet." The landlord was a tall knobby man who looked like Ichabod Crane.

"What about the shower?"

"It doesn't have one."

"I'll take it," Tim said. He forked over the cash. The room had a door, a window, and a fireplace, but Tim had no time to buy firewood. Autumn had come to Wanganui. Spring had come to Wrigley Field.

Tim was short, non-knobby, and owned no umbrella. As the rain continued to fall on Wanganui, Tim's hometown, he moved into the room. He hauled in a table, a chair, a computer, and four blankets. He plugged the computer into the phone jack. He turned it on.

The computer lit up: "Dell." "Windows." Blue dots moved across the screen.

Tim clicked "Mozilla Firefox."

He clicked "The Official Site of Major League Baseball" at mlb.com, where he paid 109.95 USD by means of American Express.

Tim was ready to watch the Chicago Cubs. At his zip code in New Zealand, twelve thousand miles from Chicago, blackout restrictions did not apply.

The next day, Tim turned on the computer and logged on to mlb.com. He clicked the icon for the Cubs game and prepared to take notes. The image of two announcers appeared on the screen. Tim recorded the starting lineup for the Cubs: Lopez, Suzuki, Gomez, Iguchi, Perez, Matsui, Sanchez, Taguchi. On the mound: Smith-Jones.

The starting lineup for the Milwaukee Brewers included Gonzalez, Iguchi, Hernandez, etc. Smith-Jones finished warming up, the first Milwaukee batter walked to the plate, and the game began.

Smith-Jones walked the first four batters. This elicited a trip to the mound by Mono Moto, manager of the Cubs. The next batter hit a hard grounder to Gomez at third, who fielded the ball and threw it to the catcher. The catcher tagged the runner and dropped the ball.

The game went on in this fashion for nine innings, and the Brewers won twenty to zero. After the game, Tim opened his website, clicked on "New Post," and typed his first story of the season:

Cubs lose

Smith-Jones gave up only 20 hits against the Milwaukee Brewers Tuesday night, but 10 of them were homers. He also allowed 18 walks. The Cubs committed 25 errors.

The Brewers won 20-0.

The Cub offense failed to keep up with the Brewers. They picked up one hit and no runs.

The Cubs play the Brewers again Wednesday night at Wrigley Field. Game time: 7:05 CT.

The next day, Tim checked his Google analytics report. Ten people had read his story.

Someone knocked. Then someone knocked again, louder this time. Tim kicked the four blankets aside and got up off the floor. He unlocked the door and pulled it open. Meg stepped inside. Water dripped from her raincoat.

"Why don't you come home?" she said. "I'm sick of coming here to see you. Everyone thinks you're crazy."

"Too busy. Too much to do. Can't leave in the middle of the season."

"Season? What season. What are you doing?" Meg was short, plump, and drunk. She did not look like Ichabod Crane.

"Meg, it's time for me to do something. It's time for me to make a difference."

"You're crazy, Tim. I wish you'd never gone to America. If you love it so much, why don't you go back?"

"They won't let me into the forty-eight contiguous states."

"Why not? What did you do?"

"I can't remember."

"Liar." Meg walked out and slammed the door so hard that it cracked the window. Tim made a note to pay the landlord 50 NZD for repairs.

He put on his clothes and his parka, walked through the rain to the coffee shop, and returned with a gallon of coffee.

Tim drank coffee and walked around the room for three hours. That afternoon, he watched the next game. Then he typed his second story.

CUBS MUST ANSWER QUESTIONS

This spring the Cubs must answer many questions.

Will they finish above .500? Will they catch the Milwaukee Brewers? Will they start well and then, like the daylilies, fade in the autumn?

And will Cub fans continue to fill Wrigley Field, regardless of how poorly the team plays? What is the mysterious attraction of Wrigley Field? What secret does it hold?

The next day, Tim checked his Google analytics report. Eight people had read the story. After the game, he typed another.

MORE QUESTIONS FOR CUBS

New questions have sprouted. Rumors fill the bleachers.

Are the Cubs for sale? Will someone buy them? Who? For how much? Why?

As the polar ice caps melt, will Lake Michigan fill Wrigley Field? Will a hole in the ozone layer form above the pitcher's mound?

Will the players refuse to play? Who will play instead? Will they relocate to Branson, Mo?

Seven people read this story.

Tim walked through the rain to confession at St. Teresa's Church. "Why can't you go back?" Father Kelly said.

"They revoked my visa."

"Why?"

"I tried to sell snow cones at Wrigley Field."

"What's wrong with that?"

"I stole the ice."

Father Kelly stared at him.

"Will God forgive me?" Tim said.

"I don't know."

❧

Tim wrote another story.

THE CRUCIAL IMPORTANCE OF MAY

In the Central Division, the Cubs are now in last place, trailing, in this order, Milwaukee, St. Louis, Pittsburgh, Cincinnati, and Houston.

The Cubs are 54 games out of first place and 30 games behind Houston.

If the Cubs hope to catch the division leaders, they will have to make their move before September 15.

Five people read this story.

Someone was pounding on the door again. Tim pushed the four blankets aside. A cold, hard rain was falling. "I'm getting a divorce," Meg shouted.

"Why?"

"You never come home."

"Why can't you wait?"

"Until when?"

"After the playoffs."

Meg slammed the door, breaking the window again. Tim made a note to pay the landlord another 50 NZD.

Tim walked through the rain to St. Teresa's Church. "I haven't been to mass since opening day," he said to Father Kelly.

"Why not?"

"Too busy."

"That's not a good reason."

"Will God forgive me?"

"Will you start going to mass again?"

"Yes."

"When?"

"After the Cubs catch the Brewers."

Tim stepped into the rain and walked back to his room. He sent an urgent e-mail to the commissioner of baseball, who, according to all reports, was tall, knobby, and looked like Ichabod Crane.

Dear Mr. Commissioner:

I feel abandoned. My wife has left me. God will not forgive me. The Immigration and Naturalization Service (AKA Immigration and Customs Enforcement [ICE]) won't let me into the forty-eight contiguous states.

What can I do? Can you help me?

Sincerely,

Timothy Billows

While waiting for a reply, he wrote his next story.

WHY DON'T I UNDERSTAND?

A Norwegian study shows that the oldest boy in a family of boys is smarter than his brothers.

This proves what I've always known. My brother is smarter than I, although neither of us is Norwegian.

My brother understands everything. I can't even understand the Chicago Cubs. Why do they always lose? Why are they so important? What secrets do they conceal?

I asked my brother these questions. He said I was an idiot.

Two people read this story. Tim received a reply from the commissioner of baseball.

Dear Mr. Billows:

You stole crushed ice at Wrigley Field in the City of Chicago.

You are an unwanted alien.

I cannot help you.

Sincerely,

Ichabod Johnson

Commissioner of Baseball

❧

Someone knocked. Tim pushed the four blankets aside, got up, and opened the door. A large man without knobs stood in the rain. "Are you Timothy Billows?" he said.

"Yes."

"These papers concern the divorce sought by your wife, Margaret Billows. Sign here please."

"I don't want a divorce."

"Signing doesn't mean you want it, only that you received the papers. Sign here."

Tim signed.

The man left, and Tim closed the door and looked at the papers. He read the first five sentences, but they made no sense.

He set the pages on the computer table and walked around the room for two hours. Then he picked up the papers and read the first five sentences again. They still made no sense.

He put on his clothes and walked through the rain to the telephone on the street corner. He stood in the rain and dialed.

"Hello."

"Hello, Meg. I wanted to—" Meg hung up. Tim stood there in the rain.

> To my faithful readers:
> This is my last story. My quest for the truth has come to an end. The Chicago Cubs will always remain life's greatest mystery. What does it mean to have faith in a team that never wins? Why do all trains stop at Wrigley Field? And why is the commissioner of baseball so obsessed with crushed ice?

The next day, Tim checked his Google analytics report. No one had read his final story.

MINUTES

DEEPWATER SKYWATCH SUPPORT GROUP
GENERAL MEETING, JUNE 10

President Alice Dinsmore called the meeting to order at 7:05 p.m. at the home of Margo Peterson. The minutes of the previous meeting were read and discussed. Charlie Floyd said the minutes were okay, but they left out his idea for an alien-abduction hall of fame right here in the city of Deepwater. He said it was a dream of his, and he didn't want to see it forgotten. The secretary said sorry and made the change. Treasurer Molly Bird reported a balance on hand of $520.

REPORTS:

CREDIT CARD COMMITTEE:

Brian Higgins reported that he was still looking for a credit card company to offer the abductee gold card. Three had turned him down, but he was still hopeful. Dinsmore said we were all behind him and keep up the good work.

SOCIAL COMMITTEE:

Kate Swift said she had scheduled the Dancemor for the UFO winter formal. The Good Time Boys will play from nine till midnight for $500, in advance, but they refuse to wear translucent white suits and oval goggles. Peterson said for $500 they should wear whatever we wanted, but Swift said they wouldn't do it.

PUBLICITY COMMITTEE:

Frank Williams said the *Deepwater Gazette* had refused to print his press release about the aliens in his neighbor's silo. Swift said the press always focused on sensationalism and overlooked serious news. Dinsmore told Williams not to get discouraged and keep up the good work.

IMPLANT COMMITTEE:

Floyd said he had received a letter from a man who had four alien implants removed this year—a wood screw, a little triangle-shaped piece of metal with a phosphorescent green glow, and two slot-machine tokens. The implant removal team at a secret clinic in Minnesota took them out. Floyd said he wants to put together a computer data base on alien implants, but he doesn't have a computer. Williams said implants were vital information and maybe the group should buy a computer, and he could type press releases on it when Floyd wasn't using it. Bird estimated that a good computer and all the stuff that goes with it would cost about $1500 and we would be $1480 short after paying the band for the winter formal. Dinsmore told Floyd to find out the exact cost of a computer and think about funding before the next meeting.

OLD BUSINESS:

Peterson asked if anyone had come up with any ideas to increase membership, in view of the fact we were down to nine members. Williams thought maybe a public service announcement for TV would help, but would cost about $50,000 to produce. Bird calculated that after paying the band we would be $49,980 short. Peterson suggested calling off the UFO winter formal and using the money for the public service announcement, but Swift said too much work had already gone into the formal. Dinsmore told the group to think about funding before the next meeting.

NEW BUSINESS:

Charlie Floyd said his daughter Louise had been impregnated by aliens again and he hoped the government would pay ADC this time and not try to pass the buck. Williams offered to write a press release, but Floyd said he didn't think that would do much good because no one would print it. Peterson said it really didn't make sense for the government to pay for something an alien had done. Swift said the FBI and the CIA were involved in a cover-up and they should pay. Floyd said if we decided to cancel the winter formal, he could use the $500, since aliens were notorious for being deadbeat dads. Swift said life had to go on despite everything and she wouldn't stand by and have the winter formal called off. Williams said we should pass a resolution demanding that the responsible party pay the expenses, whoever and wherever he was. Swift said so moved. Seconded by Peterson. Motion carried.

Higgins said he thought that Mexican goatsuckers were starting to divert public attention away from alien abductions and that that was a problem for abductees and their families. Floyd said he thought so, too, and compared it to the killer-bee scare. Swift said that was all the more reason to hold the UFO winter formal, since that would turn public attention back to the real issues. Williams offered to write a press release about goatsuckers, showing how they weren't really relevant to people's lives. Swift said good idea. Peterson said how about a resolution condemning the goatsucker scare. Boyd said so moved. Seconded by Williams. Motion carried.

SPEAKER:
Harold Bigby from California talked about the plan to build a chain of abductee retirement villas across the country, in connection with abductee annuities and mutual funds. Down the road, he sees a need for credit unions and casinos. Williams asked if Bigby needed any help with publicity, but Bigby said he had that covered and what he really needed was money for travel expenses. The talk was well received, except for the part about the money. Higgins moved to endorse Bigby's program, and Floyd seconded. Motion carried.

ADJOURNMENT:
Bird moved to adjourn. Higgins seconded. Adjourned at 8:10. Peterson served fruit punch and translucent white cookies.

—Respectfully submitted, Vicky Nordeen, Secretary

Burning Desire Romance Writers
DINNER MEETING
JUNE 19

Dressed in a lovely burgundy evening gown, Chairwoman Angela Chandler Dumont rose from her chair at the head of the long, gleaming walnut table and called the meeting to order at eight o'clock. "Ladies," she said breathlessly, "first I must thank our hostess on behalf of the group. The chilled champagne and lightly sautéed vegetables orientale were exquisite, especially in this beautiful setting in Deepwater's exclusive East End, with the moonlight streaming through the high windows with their Palladian summits. Thank you, Penelope."

Beaming with pride, Penelope Allister Gillete rose from her place at the opposite end of the table and smiled sincerely to the sound of heartfelt applause. In her saucy sailor suit with jaunty cap, Penelope looked very much like her own lively heroine, Candice Winston Rothschild, in *Mutinous Heart.*

Penelope reclaimed her chair just as waiter Luke Savage entered the room to replenish the delicate, long-stemmed glasses with chilled champagne. Dressed in skin-tight black trousers, a red-and-white-striped polo shirt, and a dark-blue beret, Luke swiftly circled the table, deftly refilling each trembling glass, his muscles rippling like a palomino's. Penelope's smile fled as her guests followed Luke's every movement, examined every sinew, probed every feature of his handsome face. "Thank you, Luke," said Penelope, her voice now as cool as the champagne. "That will be all." Luke returned the bottle to the ice pail, then strode out of the room, pausing only to close the French doors behind him. And as he did, who could have missed the faint smile playing at the corners of his strong, virile mouth.

Everyone remained motionless, enchanted by the vision that had just passed among them. Virginia Strethmor Cosgrove could neither move nor speak, although the look on her face spoke volumes of radiant, inspired prose. Finally, Chairwoman Angela Chandler Dumont, her own face still flushed with emotion, spoke to the group. "Ladies, let us now turn our attention to the manuscript for the evening, the first chapter of Virginia Strethmor Cosgrove's new novel." Virginia had by now recovered her composure and smiled warmly at Angela. "Let me begin, Virginia," said Angela, "by saying how much I enjoyed this chapter of *Desire of a Waiter*."

"I thoroughly agree," said Abigail Marquis Lafitte, the high color of her beautiful, honest face enhanced by her lovely white gown, which seemed to shimmer in the candlelight. "The hero and heroine came alive for me from the first moment they saw each other: he a poor boy trying to get ahead but stifled by his employer, a wealthy but bitter divorcée; she, the heroine, longing for his love but separated from him by the intrigues of the wealthy divorcée. You've written a wonderful beginning, Virginia. I can't wait to see the next chapter."

"Thank you, Abigail," said Angela. "Any other reactions?"

Hostess Penelope Allister Gillette cleared her throat.

"Penelope?" said Angela.

"Well, I'm certain that Abigail is quite right, but I must say that I found the premise just a little bit weak. Why would a handsome young man like Duncan fall for a simple, unattractive girl like Rosemary when his beautiful, wealthy employer, Rosalind, can offer him everything? Who's going to believe that?"

"Well," said Virginia, her steel-blue eyes now two pools of sparks, "I think any intelligent reader would believe it. Anyone with a heart beating in her breast would believe it. Only a rich old cynic would doubt it."

"Rich old cynic? Let me tell you something," said Penelope, her voice now loud and shrill.

"Ladies, please," said Angela, her face suddenly white, like new snow in a pine forest.

Penelope ignored her. "Rich old cynics, as you call them, create jobs for young men and provide dinners like this one. You didn't seem to mind the food, Virginia. I watched you eat it."

At just that moment, the French doors swung open and Luke Savage strode purposefully into the room, pushing a cart on which sat a gleaming silver coffee pot with matching creamer and sugar bowl, along with ten delft cups and saucers. The visitors all turned and beamed at Luke as he came toward them. A collective sigh rose like mist from the table.

"Luke!" said Penelope. "It's too late for coffee. Get out."

Without missing a step, Luke pushed the cart through a wide, smooth arc and out the door. The ladies watched sadly as he turned, closed the French doors, and disappeared down the hallway with the cart.

A long period of silence followed this exit. Finally, Chairwoman Angela Chandler Dumont sighed deeply. "Penelope," she said, "I could have used a good cup of coffee."

"Well you won't get it here," said Penelope. "The coffee here comes at a high price." She took off her sailor's cap and threw it on the floor.

The meeting adjourned at eight-thirty. Several of the ladies went to Bob's Diner for coffee.

Respectfully and sincerely submitted,

Jessica Bourne Covington, Secretary-Treasurer

SKUNK RIVER MOTORCYCLE CLUB

MONTHLY MEETING

JULY 1

President Earl Tharp banged a pool cue on the bar at nine o'clock and called the meeting to order. The noise caused Fred Porter to spin around so fast on his bar stool that he knocked over three bottles of Old Style. Everyone started yelling, and old man Schwartz came back from the front of the bar and said keep it down, there are people trying to watch the wrestling on TV. Earl said don't worry about it and told the secretary to read the minutes of the last meeting. The secretary said they got lost, so he couldn't read them. Mike Turbin said the secretary couldn't read to begin with, but Earl told him to shut up so we could get this over with because he had work to do. Someone woke up Marv Griner and he read the treasurer's report. He said we were $600 in debt for 15 kegs of Old Style. Earl told him to find the money somewhere. Marv said where? Earl said that was his problem and let's get on with the meeting so he could go home and finish grinding his valves. Marv said okay and went back to sleep.

REPORTS
BEER COMMITTEE
Billy Fargo said the committee was trying to decide between Old Style and Hollenbeck's for the Harley Days Picnic. He said Hollenbeck's cost less but tasted like tom cat p__s. Earl asked how much money he'd collected so far. Billy said $6.32, and Earl said better get the Hollenbeck's. He said Billy should talk to Marv, since he was the treasurer and always knew where to get his hands on some money. Marv was still asleep, so Earl poked him with the cue stick and told him to start thinking about getting money for the picnic. Marv said he'd try to borrow some and went back to sleep.

WHISKEY COMMITTEE
Tucker Boyle said his committee had tried to get a case of Jack Daniels for the Harley Days Picnic, but a deputy sheriff had pulled up just at the wrong time and they were lucky to get away. Earl said they should be more careful next time. Tucker said they were careful this time but it wasn't easy getting into a warehouse in the dark with chicken s__t deputies snooping around all the time. Earl said it wasn't supposed to be easy and just do it. Tucker started to say something else, but Earl banged the cue stick on the bar and yelled just get off your a_s and do it! Old man Schwartz walked back and said I told you guys to keep it down! Earl said okay, okay.

WINE COMMITTEE
Dutch Martin said he got a real good deal on three cases of Thunderbird at the Hy-Vee. The manager promised it at $4 a case if Dutch could guarantee the store wouldn't burn down like the one in Des Moines.

Dutch said he could and now he had the three cases locked up in the back of his van. Mike Turbin said he didn't like Thunderbird and why didn't Dutch get something good like muscatel. Dutch said Thunderbird was all they had and if Mike didn't like it he could get his own d__n wine. Mike said maybe he'd just do that and gave Dutch the f____r. Then Dutch gave Mike the f____r and said drop d__d! Earl said keep it down idiots, this is the only bar in town where they'll let us have our meetings.

COCAINE COMMITTEE

Mike Turbin said he couldn't get any more cocaine from Wilson Carter on account of Wilson being in the hospital with knife and gunshot wounds from a domestic dispute, so it didn't look like we'd have any coke for the Harley Days Picnic. Dutch Martin said Carter wasn't the only coke dealer and Mike should get off his lazy a_s and find someone else. Mike said someone else might be a cop. Dutch said not to be such a w__p. Mike said I'll show you who's a w__p and started toward Dutch, but Earl hit him over the head with the cue stick. It broke the cue, but Earl put it back in the rack and pretended nothing had happened. Tucker Boyle poured a pitcher of beer on Mike's face and he woke up as good as new, though he couldn't remember anything that had happened in the last six months.

OLD BUSINESS

Dutch Martin reminded the group that Torch Bailey was still in jail on $400,000 bond for burning down the Hy-Vee in Des Moines. Earl said that was just the way it always was and why didn't they let him out and look for some real criminals. Dutch said that's right but what about the $400,000. On account of Torch's record, no bail bondsman would put up a dime for him. Earl said that's a real shame. Billy Fargo said the shame was that Torch was so stupid that he just stood there like he always does watching the fire while the police took pictures of the crowd. Dutch said that wasn't the point. We had to raise the bail. Earl asked Luke Savage if he could get any more money out of the old bat he was playing house with. Luke said not that kind of money. Earl grunted, then got a new pool cue from the rack and woke Marv up to tell him we needed more money. Marv said piece of cake and went back to sleep.

NEW BUSINESS

Tucker Boyle said we should try to recruit more members for the club. Counting Torch Bailey, we now had five members in jail and hardly anyone left on the outside. Dutch said who would want to join? Tucker said my brother for one. Dutch said oh c__p, not another Boyle. Then you'll want to get all the rest of your brothers in. Tucker said so what. Dutch said because one Boyle is enough and we have enough trouble as it is without bringing in a whole family of idiots. Tucker said who you calling idiots you m_d face. Dutch said you and your idiot brothers you d_rt face. Earl raised the cue and said s__t up before I have to break another cue stick.

ADJOURNMENT

Old man Schwartz kicked everyone out at nine-thirty.

Fred Porter, Secretary

Deepwater City Council

WEEKLY MEETING

JULY 8, CITY HALL

Mayor Michael O'Neill called the meeting to order at 8:10. Also present were Councilmen O'Brien, O'Connor, O'Gorman, O'Hara, O'Kelly, O'Malley, O'Mara, O'Reilly, and O'Toole. Absent: O'Keefe and O'Leary.

REPORTS:

CULTURAL DIVERSITY COMMITTEE:

O'Connor said that all council members had agreed to wear sombreros to a future meeting of the council. He also stated that Herman Schmidt would show his slides of the Rhine Valley the next Saturday afternoon at the City Library, Parnell Room. This would be followed by a public reading of her "Italian Sketches" by Penelope Alister Gillette.

O'Toole asked if the committee included alien abductors in its definition of cultural diversity. O'Connor said they did not, but they would in the future. O'Brien asked if that meant that aliens would have the right to vote. Because if it did, he'd need more yard signs for the next election. O'Connor said he hadn't thought about that and wondered what the city attorney would say. Mayor O'Neill reminded him that City Attorney Bridget O'Donoghue had run off with the Skunk River motorcycle gang and no one knew if she was coming back.

MIRACLE ABATEMENT COMMITTEE:

O'Gorman said that the reports of Christ images on tree stumps were getting worse. The streets were clogged with cars, people were parking on the lawns, dogs were making a mess, and vendors were setting up wherever they wanted and none of them bothered to buy a license.

O'Kelly said maybe it was time for a stump-removal ordinance. Mayor O'Neill told him to write it up and the council would give it first consideration at the next meeting. O'Kelly said he wished he could ask the city attorney for help, but he'd do the best he could. He also said people probably wouldn't like the expense of having to remove their stumps, but he'd write it up anyway.

OLD BUSINESS:

Mayor O'Neill said negotiations with the Near-Death Coalition had broken down entirely. The coalition continued to demand that anyone who had a near-death experience was entitled to an official death certificate. The county medical examiner refused to consider it and now the coalition wanted the city to get into the death certificate business. O'Mara said maybe the city could dummy something up on good-quality paper and sell them for fifteen or twenty dollars apiece and use the money to fund the stump-removal ordinance. The mayor said that was an excellent idea and told O'Mara to work with O'Kelly on it.

O'Malley reported that his investigation of comet survival strategies had led him to a company called Comet React, Inc. For $5000, the company would prepare a municipal comet survival plan. For an additional monthly fee, Comet React, Inc., would also manage the plan, or the city could manage it itself. The advantage of the city doing it would be a considerable savings to the taxpayers. The disadvantage would be that nobody in Deepwater knew anything about comets.

Mayor O'Neill said that no matter who managed the plan, it was time for the city to do something about comet survival. All the TV stations were talking about comets. The newspapers were full of comets. The people were worried and wanted something done. O'Reilly asked exactly how much it would cost to hire Comet React to manage the survival plan. O'Malley said he asked about that, but Luke Savage, the sales rep for Comet React, had been vague about it. Mayor O'Neill said we had to have a ballpark figure to go on and that O'Malley should press Savage for some numbers and report back at the next meeting. O'Brien asked if this was the same Luke Savage who used to be a lighting-rod salesman. O'Malley said he didn't know.

NEW BUSINESS:

O'Hara said he'd had many complaints from the public and he thought it was time for the council to take up the skateboard issue. There were no regulations for skateboards, and kids were riding them wherever they felt like it, and people were sick of having to risk death or injury just to walk down the sidewalk. O'Gorman said he agreed completely and that the damn things should be outlawed and he'd be happy to help write the ordinance. O'Mara said we might run into questions of constitutionality if we tried to ban them altogether. It might be better to regulate them by establishing a licensing fee and designating an area where kids could use them. The revenue could then be used for the stump-removable program.

O'Hara said all that was just fine, but exactly what area would we designate for skateboard use. O'Mara suggested the last block of Shamrock Street. O'Hara said no way, José. I live on that block. Why don't you use your own block and see how you like it? Mayor O'Neill said we shouldn't get the cart before the horse. What we needed was the city attorney's opinion on the constitutionality of banning skateboards altogether. O'Mara asked what good it was to have a city attorney if she was never there when we needed her. O'Neill said the council should talk about the skateboard issue again at the next meeting and he'd try to get the city attorney back to work by then.

QUESTIONS FROM THE PUBLIC:
There being no further new business, the mayor asked for questions from the public. Henry Beane of 521 Parnell Street stood up and said that as usual the council was wasting its time on trivialities and ignoring the most important issue altogether. Mayor O'Neill asked him just what the most important issue might be and Beane said goatsuckers, Mexican goatsuckers. The Mayor said may I remind you that the City of Deepwater is a thousand miles north of Mexico. Beane said he didn't care. Two of his goats had been killed by goatsuckers in the last week. O'Neill asked how he knew what killed them. Beane said because they didn't have any blood left in them. O'Gorman said it didn't matter what killed them; the fact was that a city ordinance prohibited the raising of sheep or goats inside the city limits. Beane said he didn't raise them inside the city limits. He had fifty acres a mile north of town. Then you came to the wrong place, O'Neill said. He said Beane needed to talk to the county board of supervisors. The council handled goatsucker complaints inside the city limits only, and it didn't want a jurisdiction controversy with the county, especially without a city attorney on board.

ADJOURNMENT:

There being no other questions from the public, O'Gorman moved to adjourn. O'Kelly seconded. Motion carried. Meeting adjourned at 9:15.

    Signed: Michael O'Neill, Mayor
            Colleen O'Neill, City Clerk

Gabby Hayes Fan Club
GENERAL MEETING
JULY 10

President Hank Nordquist called the meeting to order at 12:01 p.m. in the balcony of the Rialto King Theater in downtown Deepwater, pausing to remind the group that the matinee would begin in one hour. Secretary Belle Chan read the minutes of the previous meeting, though not without interruption, as Slim Rothstein arrived late and immediately dropped six bags of popcorn in the second row. "Con sarn it," he said, "do we have any more money in the popcorn fund?" Treasurer Tex Taragano said we didn't. The secretary finished reading the minutes, which were approved as read. The treasurer reported a balance on hand of three dollars, plus an inventory of two thousand Gabby Hayes T-shirts.

REPORTS:
MISSION STATEMENT COMMITTEE:

Calamity Fay Godunov reported that the committee had completed work on the Gabby Hayes Fan Club Mission Statement, which she then read aloud:

"The Mission of the Gabby Hayes Fan Club is to create greater public recognition of the importance of Gabby Hayes in motion picture history. Furthermore, the Mission is to help members obtain Gabby Hayes artifacts and paraphernalia. Moreover, the Mission is to increase the value of Gabby Hayes artifacts and paraphernalia."

"Any comments or questions?" said President Nordquist after Chairwoman Godunov had read the statement. "Sounds real good," said

Shorty Aman. "I have a Gabby Hayes belt buckle, solid brass, in mint condition. I'll let it go for fifty dollars." "Give you twenty-five," said Cookie Mitsumasa. "Gentlemen, this isn't the right time for business," President Nordquist said. "We're considering a very important issue." "I move we accept the Mission Statement as read," said Aman. "Second," said Mitsumasa. "Any discussion?" said Nordquist. There was none. "All those in favor of the motion say—" Just as the group was about to vote, Slim Rothstein spilled six cups of Coca-Cola in Calamity Fay Godunov's lap. "Dad-blame it," Rothstein said. Five minutes later, after the mess had been cleaned up, the motion passed without opposition.

PUBLICITY COMMITTEE:
After selling his Gabby Hayes belt buckle for $35.00, Shorty Aman reported that his committee had contacted the Roy Rogers-Dale Evans Museum in Victorville, California, about the museum's lack of respect for Gabby Hayes and related artifacts and paraphernalia. "We told them it was insulting that there was a big statue of Trigger at the museum but no statue at all of Gabby Hayes. We said it made no sense to publicize a horse more than a loyal, trusted sidekick." "Darn tootin'," Slim Rothstein said.

"Anyway," Aman continued, "we demanded that the management take down the Trigger statue and replace it with a statue of Gabby Hayes. "What did they say?" President Nordquist asked. "No deal, no way, not a chance," Aman said. "We threatened to organize a nationwide boycott, but they just hung up on us."

CONFERENCE COMMITTEE:
Committee Chairman Cookie Mitsumasa stated that plans were progressing for the First Annual Gabby Hayes Conference and Exhibition at the Deepwater Junior College. A number of presentations had already been scheduled:
1. Gabby Hayes as Cultural Icon.
2. Gabby as Role Model.

3. Gabby Hayes: The Legend and the Legacy.

4. Trends in Gabby Hayes Artifacts and Paraphernalia.

5. Counterfeit Artifacts: Scourge and Scandal.

Mitsumasa said the committee had invited Arnold Schwarzenegger to deliver the keynote address, but he had turned them down. They were now going to invite Jesse Ventura. Nordquist asked how many people had registered for the conference. Mitsumasa said no one yet, but he still expected a big turnout.

OLD BUSINESS:

Tex Taragano asked if the group had given any more thought to the idea of sending a delegation to Gabby Hayes Day in Wellsville, New York, which, he reminded everyone, was Gabby's hometown. He said we, at the very least, should enter someone in the Gabby Hayes Look-Alike Contest. But Calamity Fay Godunov said, "The only person in Deepwater who looks like Gabby Hayes is Elsie Murdoch, and she's too busy at the Ready Mix plant to go anywhere." Nordquist said maybe next year.

Lucky Luke Savage reminded the group that he still had over a thousand antique Gabby Hayes mustache cups that he'd be glad to sell to the club for half what he paid for them, and the cups were still as good as new. Aman said they looked a little too new for him. Savage replied, "They're not fakes! I bought them from a warehouse in Los Angeles where they'd been stored for fifty years." "Probably more like fifty minutes," Aman said. Taragano said it didn't make any difference how long the cups had been in the warehouse, since the club only had three dollars in the treasury and two thousand Gabby Hayes T-shirts in inventory. "Would you trade the cups for the shirts?" he asked. "No," Savage said. "Would you sell them for three dollars?" Everybody looked at Savage. "Sold," he said.

NEW BUSINESS:

Slim Rothstein spilled a bucket of Milk Duds over the balcony rail, and a bunch of kids downstairs started throwing them back. "Dad-burn kids," Rothstein said. "What in the Sam Hill makes 'em act like that?"

ADJOURNMENT:

With the matinee about to start, Aman moved to adjourn. Seconded by Mitsumasa. Meeting adjourned at 1:00 p.m. Everyone stayed for the 1946 classic, *My Pal Trigger*.

Respectfully submitted,

Belle Chan, Secretary

THE BAND THAT BEGUILES

Lois lit a Benson & Hedges with her Jean-Paul Cuistot cigarette lighter and inhaled deeply. "Why do you want to drag him all the way to New York just to buy a pair of shoes?" she said.

Her long red hair and lacquered nails looked especially unattractive to Peter this morning. "You can't get a decent pair of shoes for a baby in these New Jersey shopping centers," he said. "There's a good shoe store just off of Union Square."

"Union Square!" She said it like an epithet. "You always want to go to Union Square. You're living in the past."

"You forget that I'm a history teacher. The past is important."

"Don't give me another one of your high-school lectures."

Peter finished his coffee and set the cup in the sink. "Lois, your attitude toward this project is giving me a cramp in the balls."

"Don't talk that way in front of Sammy."

Sammy stuck a fistful of oatmeal into his mouth.

"It won't hurt him," Peter said.

"You know how he repeats things," Lois said. "It would be embarrassing if he said something like that in the wrong place." She scraped what was left of her scrambled eggs into the garbage can.

"Like where?" Peter said.

"Like at Flo's house."

"Flo is a moron."

"Peter!"

"The woman annoys me."

Sammy held his dish out at arm's length and carefully dropped it on the floor.

"I don't care if she does," Lois said. "You should watch what you say in front of Sammy."

"Uh-oh," Sammy said, looking over the edge of his highchair at the pool of oatmeal on the floor.

"If we don't get going, we'll never catch the train," Peter said.

"Catch a train," Sammy said.

"Now I've got to clean up this mess," Lois said. She snuffed out her cigarette in her Pierre Dulac ashtray and tore a couple of paper towels off the roll.

"Catch a train," Sammy said with more force.

"Will you drive us to the train or not?" Peter said.

"Oh, I suppose so, if you've got your heart set on Union Square." She wiped up the oatmeal and threw the paper towels into the garbage can.

"I just want to get him a good pair of shoes."

"Shoes," Sammy said. "Catch a train."

Lois dressed Sammy while Peter got the diaper bag ready. They strapped Sammy into his baby seat and started for the station. Lois drove with appalling slowness.

"Can't you drive any faster?" Peter said.

"There's a speed limit here, you know."

They crossed the bridge. "Red Bank. Some town to be broke in," Peter said.

"You've been watching too many Bogart movies," Lois said.

The track was closed for repairs between Matawan and South Amboy. Peter carried Sammy from the train to the bus and held him on his lap while they vibrated north.

They stood on the brick platform at South Amboy, watching a train back up to the station. "Catch a train," Sammy said. "Daddy coming?"

"That's right," Peter said. "We'll catch the train."

A fat man in a T-shirt bore down on them. Peter looked the other way. Too late.

"Hi there," said the fat man, taking a soggy cigar out of his mouth. He set a brown shopping bag on the platform. "What's your name, Mister Engineer?" He tugged on one of the straps of Sammy's Oshkosh B'Gosh overalls.

"Can you tell the man your name?" Peter said.

"Nose," Sammy said, putting his finger on the tip of his nose.

"I'll tell you my name if you'll tell me yours," said the fat man. "Look, here's a quarter."

"Penny," Sammy said, grabbing the coin.

"I'm Ben Stiles. What's your name?"

"Nose," Sammy said.

"Remember me?" said the fat man, looking down at Peter. His breath reeked of bourbon and cigars.

"Sure," Peter said, glancing at his watch. "Big-band leader."

"So you remember me, huh?"

"Sure."

"I'm working in New York with Jack Roy."

"Is that so?"

"We're at Rico's on Thirty-Ninth Street."

"You don't say?"

"Go shoes," Sammy said.

They let the fat man get on first, then took a seat ten rows behind. The windows showed no signs of ever having been washed. Perth Amboy passed in a gray blur. Elizabeth slumbered behind a muddy smudge.

Sammy played with a string of wooden beads while Peter read a story in the *Times* about a twelve-car accident on the Cross-Bronx Expressway. The conductor, a handsome Mediterranean, began conversing with Sammy. "How's the big boy?" he said. "You like the train?"

"Like a train," Sammy said.

"That a boy. Keep liking that train."

Peter closed the paper. "See that fat guy up there?" he said.

"Him? Oh yeah."

"He said he was Ben Stiles."

"Yeah, that's who he is, all right, Ben Stiles." He looked back at Sammy. "That's quite the boy you got there," he said.

The fat man got off in Newark. Five hours later, Sammy and Peter passed through in the opposite direction.

"No shoes," said Sammy.

"No shoes," said Peter.

A short man in a plaid suit got on in Perth Amboy and sat down across the aisle. Sammy stood at the window, trying to see through the grime.

"See the wedding?" said the man in plaid.

"Wedding?" Peter said.

"Yeah, the wedding. You know, the prince, over in Europe."

"I wasn't invited."

"Doesn't matter. It was on TV," the man said.

"Is that a fact?"

"Sure. Saw it myself." He took an apple from his pocket and began polishing it on his pant leg.

"Seems a little ostentatious."

"How's that?"

"It seems a little showy, getting married on television."

"Merry," Sammy said.

"Oh, they have to do that," the man said. "He'll be a king someday." He took a big bite out of the apple and chewed thoughtfully.

The train lurched across a switch, and Sammy fell into Peter's lap. "I don't think I'd want to get married on TV," Peter said.

"Ride a merry," Sammy said.

"We'll ride the merry-go-round tomorrow," Peter said.

"It was quite a show."

"Bet it was. Sorry I missed it."

"There'll be reruns," the man said, taking another bite.

"Who's the happy bride?" Peter said.

The man chewed and swallowed. "Lady somebody-or-other. I can't remember."

"Did she pass the VD test?"

"What?"

"Did she pass the VD test? What if she's got the clap?"

"Clap a daddy," Sammy said. He began pounding Peter on the head with both hands.

"I didn't hear about that," the man said, examining a bruise on the apple. "It wasn't on TV."

Sammy and Peter got off at the deserted station in Red Bank and took a cab home. Lois looked up from a copy of *People* and glared at Peter as he came through the door.

"Lois, I've got some bad news," Peter said.

"What?" she said, setting her gin and tonic on the coffee table.

"The young prince has gonorrhea."

"Peter, you're rotten." She dropped the magazine on the floor and crossed her arms.

"You don't seem interested in his majesty's medical problems," Peter said. He sat down on the couch, and Sammy crawled up beside him.

"Flo called."

"How can you be so insensitive to the heartaches of royalty?"

"Flo called," Lois repeated.

"What did old Flo have to offer?" Peter said. Sammy grabbed him around the neck and put his thumb on the right lens of Peter's horn-rimmed glasses.

"She saw you with a woman on the boardwalk in Asbury Park."

"Park," Sammy said. "Go park."

"When did this incident occur?"

"About ten-thirty this morning."

"I'm afraid that's impossible. At ten-thirty I was on the way to New York with Ben Stiles." Sammy began bouncing up and down the couch.

"She saw you again this afternoon with the same woman, about an hour ago."

"Equally impossible. An hour ago I was discussing the prince's social disease with a well-dressed gentleman on the train."

"Flo saw you."

"Where did this second sighting occur?"

"On the same boardwalk in Asbury Park," Lois said, getting up from the rocking chair.

"Park," Sammy said. "Ride a merry."

"Flo's spending entirely too much time on that boardwalk," Peter said.

"How could you, Peter? And you had Sammy with you. Flo saw you letting her hold him." Lois tugged at the elastic waistband of her monogrammed jogging shorts and sat back down.

"I'm innocent."

"Flo said you kissed her while she was holding him."

"This whole thing is insulting," Peter said.

"What do you mean?" Lois said.

"I would never conduct an affair in Asbury Park."

"This isn't funny, Peter. Flo saw you." She lit a Virginia Slim and blew a stream of smoke across the room.

"Flo is mistaken. I was on the train."

"Prove it!" Lois said.

"Cramp a balls," Sammy said.

"See this quarter?" Peter said. He laid it on the kitchen table beside a glass cocker spaniel. Sammy was sleeping with two bears and a dump truck in the bedroom directly overhead. Lois began stroking her hair with her Marcel Cordon hairbrush. "It was given to our son by Ben Stiles at the same time that Flo claims to have seen me with a beautiful woman on the boardwalk."

"Flo didn't say she was beautiful," Lois said.

"Flo has no eye for detail."

"Then you admit it!" she said, lowering the brush.

"I admit nothing. I was riding through the lovely New Jersey country-side with Ben Stiles."

"Who the hell is Ben Stiles?"

"Not so loud. Sammy will hear you."

"Peter, you bastard, who's Ben Stiles?" She banged the hairbrush down on the table.

"Don't you remember Ben Stiles? Ben Stiles and the Band That Beguiles?"

"What?"

"Ben Stiles and the Band That Beguiles. That's what they used to call themselves."

"I'm leaving you, Peter. I'm taking Sammy and leaving first thing in the morning."

"Don't do that."

"Why not?"

"Because you'd be making a mistake, and we should never make mistakes. Flo is incorrect. Flo is in error. I did not commit adultery on the boardwalk. I went to New York with Sammy."

"I don't believe you," she said.

"I can prove it," he said.

"How?"

"I'll call Mr. Stiles and ask him to verify my story. I'm sure he'll do it. He was very gracious, even gave Sammy this quarter."

"Go ahead and call him." She got up, brushed some cigarette ashes off the sleeve of her Jacques Plier bathrobe, and mixed a gin gimlet. Peter thumbed through the pages of the Manhattan telephone book until he found the number.

"Rico's," a woman's voice said.

"Hello. I'm trying to get in touch with someone who's playing there."

"I'm sorry, but we don't accept calls for our performers."

"It's a matter of the utmost gravity," Peter said.

"I'm sorry."

"Lives may be ruined if I don't get through."

The woman paused. "I'll let you talk to the manager," she said. The phone went mute for a few seconds. Lois sat down, lit a Salem Light, and picked up a copy of *Us* magazine.

"Hello," a male voice said.

"Hello," Peter said. "I'm trying to get hold of Ben Stiles. It's extremely urgent."

"Who?"

"Ben Stiles."

Silence from the other end.

"You know, Ben Stiles and the Band That Beguiles?" Peter said. "He's playing there with Jack Roy."

"Oh, Jack Roy."

"That's right."

"He's playing here tonight."

"I know." Peter drummed his fingers on the telephone stand.

"But I don't know anything about Ben Stiles," the man said.

"I really need to get in touch with him," Peter said. "Is there anyone else who might know where he is?"

"Why don't you call Abe Greenspan? He used to run a club on Forty-Second Street. He knows everyone."

Peter dialed another number in Manhattan. Lois drew on the cigarette and exhaled through her nose.

"Hello."

"Hello, Mister Greenspan."

"Yes."

"I'm trying to locate Ben Stiles."

"You're not the only one. Does he owe you money?"

"No, it's not that," Peter said. "I met him while I was waiting for a train this morning. He said he was working at Rico's with Jack Roy."

"Ben Stiles hasn't worked with anyone for years," Mr. Greenspan said.

"What about his band?"

"It no longer beguiles."

"Why not?"

"It no longer exists."

"I see."

"What do you want with Stiles?"

"I talked to him in South Amboy this morning. He can prove I wasn't committing adultery in Asbury Park."

"Call Martin Coppersmith. He was Stiles' agent about fifteen or twenty years ago."

Another call to New York. Never mind the cost, Peter thought. Lois pushed the magazine aside and glowered at him through a cloud of smoke.

"Ben Stiles? I haven't seen him for twenty years," Mr. Coppersmith said.

"Do you know where he lives?"

"The last I heard he was living in Newark."

"Newark!" Peter shouted.

"What's so exciting about that?" Mr. Coppersmith said.

"It means it *was* Stiles. He got off the train in Newark. Mr. Coppersmith, this proves I wasn't in Asbury Park."

"Glad to hear it."

"Do you know his phone number?"

"He doesn't have one."

"Do you know his address?"

"No, sorry. All I know about him is that he drinks too much and he owes me five thousand dollars."

"How am I going to find him?"

"That's a question I've often asked myself. I understand he likes to hang around train stations on the North Jersey Coast Line giving quarters to little kids."

"A real philanthropist," Peter said.

"I guess so," Mr. Coppersmith said.

Peter hung up and headed toward the door.

"Where're you going?" Lois said. She stood up and started around the table.

"I'm going to clear my name," he said, stumbling over Sammy's Happy Apple.

"You can't fool me, Peter. You're just planning to meet your lover."

"This is a question of personal honor, Lois. I *have* to prove my innocence."

"This is ridiculous," Lois said.

"Goodbye," Peter said.

Peter walked the length of the train, looking for a window that would admit light. It was the third day of his search, and he'd been at it for seven hours. So far today, Stiles had failed to appear in Manasquan, Spring Lake, Belmar, Bradley Beach, Asbury Park, Allenhurst, Elberon, Long Branch, and Little Silver. Peter's optimism was beginning to wane.

He took a seat next to a window that transmitted vague images of boxcars, oil refineries, and empty warehouses. Two women sat down in front of him. One wore a polka-dot blouse with an orange skirt, the other a green ensemble. They began discussing a mutual chum.

"If she doesn't like people, she won't last a week," said the lady in green.

"That's what I told her," said her friend. "You've got to have a lot of personality to work at Wal-Mart."

Peter rode through Red Bank and got off in Middletown. An hour passed. No Stiles.

He got back on and rode to Matawan, where the bus carried him to South Amboy and another train. Five minutes later, he stepped briskly off the train at Perth Amboy and collided with a fat man carrying a brown paper bag.

"Ben Stiles!" Peter said.

"Who're you?" Stiles said suspiciously.

"I've been looking for you for three days."

Stiles drew back. "What do you want?"

"I need you to testify for me."

"Get out of the way. I'll miss the train."

"I talked to you last Friday in South Amboy," Peter said, following Stiles back onto the train. "You gave my son, Sammy, a quarter."

"I've never seen you before in my life."

"You've got to help me restore my reputation. My good name is at stake."

"Leave me alone."

Stiles took a seat. Peter hovered.

"All you have to do is tell my wife you saw me. She thinks I was getting some nooky on the boardwalk."

"You're crazy. Leave me alone or I'll call the cops."

Peter retreated to the rear of the car. The train swayed through Woodbridge and Avenel without pause and was about to start up after stopping at Rahway when Stiles leapt up and rushed out the door.

Peter ran out just in time to see Stiles tottering across the platform. The old fool's probably going to dole out a roll of quarters, Peter thought. Instead, Stiles walked away from the station and down the street. Peter followed at a safe distance.

Stiles turned a corner and went into a bar. Peter waited thirty minutes and was about to go in for a look when Stiles came out and walked on down the street. Peter trailed along about a block behind as Stiles went around another corner, passed an antique store full of glass miniatures, and turned in at a drive-in bank.

Stiles waited patiently behind two Hondas, a Fiat, a Toyota, and a Volkswagen. Peter watched from the sidewalk, ready to step out of sight behind a tree. When Stiles reached the window, the teller counted out a hundred dollars in quarters and seven hundred dollars in twenty dollar bills.

With his wallet stuffed with bills and his paper bag heavy with quarters, Stiles puffed away from the bank and down the street to another bar. Peter bought a hot dog at a café across from the bar and sat down beside a window to wait for Stiles to come out.

Sixty minutes later, Peter was finishing his second Bromo-Seltzer when Stiles emerged. Now's my chance, Peter thought. He went out the door, trotted across the street, and caught up with Stiles, who'd weaved about twenty feet from the door.

"Hello, Mister Stiles. How nice to run into you again."

Stiles jerked around and knocked over a trash can. "I though I told you to leave me alone," he said.

"I wanted to thank you again for the quarter you gave Sammy," Peter said. "It's probably the beginning of a great financial success story. You know how it goes with young people nowadays. First a lemonade stand, and before long a new hamburger chain with singing fry cooks."

"Go away."

"Don't you want to hear about Sammy's good fortune?"

"No."

"Mister Coppersmith hinted at your aloofness, but I never expected this."

"Who?"

"Martin Coppersmith. Remember him?"

"Never heard of him." Stiles blew his nose on a large red handkerchief.

"He pointed out an interesting statistic. He said you owed him five thousand dollars."

"So what?"

"He implied that he'd like to have it back."

"I don't have it," Stiles said. "I'm a poor man." He started to turn away.

"You didn't look poor at that bank back there," Peter said. "The teller counted out eight hundred dollars without stopping for breath."

"You been following me, you little rat."

"I'll bet you've got money tucked away in every bank on the North Jersey Coast Line." Peter clasped his hands together and leaned forward. "You'd have to with your generous sponsorship of the young."

"Banks aren't safe. You can't put all your money in just one."

"All what money? You said you were poor."

"I am. That's why I can't afford to take chances."

"I'm sure Mister Coppersmith would be interested in learning about your careful banking procedures," Peter said, stroking his chin. "I'll have to put him in touch with you."

"Why're you doing this?" Stiles said.

"I gather you owe money to several other people, too. They'd probably like a nice chat with you after Mister Coppersmith gets done."

"Those people will soak me for every dime."

"At least."

"Do I look rich? Look at these clothes."

"Nice disguise. I'd smear a little dirt on the T-shirt, though."

"I'd like to batter your head in."

Peter stepped out of battering range. "You'd probably like it if I didn't tell all those people where you keep your scholarship funds, wouldn't you?"

"All right," Stiles said, "what do you want from me?"

Peter told him.

"Wasn't it nice of Mr. Stiles to come all the way down here?" Peter said. He and Lois watched from the door as Stiles careened down the sidewalk to the taxi.

"Yes, it was," Lois said, "but I didn't expect him to finish the bottle when I offered him a drink."

"Oh, you know how it is with these musicians. They like to keep the blood fresh."

"He doesn't look very well off. Maybe we should've given him some money."

"I offered to buy him dinner, but he wouldn't hear of it."

"Well, it was nice of him to come anyway," she said.

"And he was glad to do it after I explained the situation," Peter said.

"I'm sorry I didn't believe you, Peter, but your story was so farfetched." They walked away from the door.

"I understand completely."

Lois picked up her martini. "I'll try not to be so suspicious in the future." She squeezed his hand and gave him a peck on the cheek.

"In the future, it won't make any difference," he said.

"Why not?"

"Because I'm leaving. I'm moving out."

Lois stared. "Moving out! Why?"

"I have a girlfriend who lives near Union Square. I'm moving in with her."

"Peter, you idiot, this doesn't make sense. If you were going to leave anyway, why did you go to all that trouble to find Ben Stiles?"

"I had to clear my name. I don't want anyone thinking I'm the kind of person who hangs around Asbury Park."

Lois sat down in the rocking chair and lit a Merit Ultra Light. Peter started for the door. "You're crazy, Peter," she said. "It'll be a relief to see you go."

"I knew you'd see the advantages," he said.

"What shall I tell Sammy?"

Peter paused on the threshold. He looked down the street, then back at Lois. "I'll see him this weekend. Just tell him I'm still looking for a good pair of shoes."

CANTALOUPES

Rennie sits on her couch, her hands folded in her lap, her eyes closed. The sound of a male voice comes out of her CD player. "Let your mind go blank," the voice says. "Free your thoughts of all extraneous influences." Rennie lets her mind go blank. Her thoughts repel all extraneous influences.

"Imagine that your brain is a ripe cantaloupe," the voice says. "Imagine that you're holding a gleaming silver knife. Grasp the cantaloupe with one hand and slice it down the middle. Separate the two halves, and suspend them in the air against a blue background." Rennie slices and suspends her imaginary cantaloupe.

"Both halves of your cantaloupe now begin to pulse with an orange glow. But as you watch them, the right half grows larger while the other half grows smaller. As it grows, the right side pulses more and more intensely while the pulsations from the left side grow weaker and weaker.

"Your brain is now primed for maximum creativity. No matter what your art form may be, your right brain is ready to produce. As the glowing right half of your cantaloupe illuminates your thoughts, let your imagination run free. Your potential is infinite. Nothing can hold you back."

The sound of waves breaking on a beach replaces the sound of the man's voice. With the right half of her cantaloupe pulsing, Rennie waits for creative thoughts to enter her mind. The waves continue to break. The right half continues to pulse.

A minute passes. Two minutes. Five minutes.

The phone rings.

Rennie opens her eyes, turns off the waves, and picks up the receiver. "Hello," she says.

"Rennie Decker?" a male voice says.

"Yes."

"Hi. I'm Gary Fargo, calling for Mindgrowth Systems. How're you today?" The man's voice sounds like a television Baptist's.

"Just fine," Rennie says. "I was kind of busy."

"I'll bet you were, a creative person like you. And in fact, that's why I called. I knew that as a subscriber to *Creativity Today*, you'd want to take advantage of our new offer. Have you heard about our right-brain augmentation system? I'm sure you have."

"I don't think so."

"Really? I'm surprised to hear that."

"Well, I'm not sure."

"It's used by many of today's most successful artists."

"Oh yes. Now I remember."

"I thought so. Well let me fill you in on the details of our new offer. Rennie, as you already know, our right-brain augmentation system increases your creativity while you sleep. It's a proven system, but up until now the cost has been too high for all but the very wealthy. And that's something that's always bothered us here at Mindgrowth. We don't think it's fair, and I'll bet you agree, don't you?"

"I see what you mean."

"I knew you would. And now we've done something about it. Using the latest technology, we've made this product economical enough for the general public.

Rennie, I think you're gonna like what I have to tell you."

"Oh?"

"That's right. A system that used to cost over ten thousand dollars can now be yours for only nineteen dollars and ninety-five cents, plus shipping and handling. Rennie, I won't waste your time telling you what a great product this is. You already know that. But I'll bet you didn't know how reasonable the cost would be, did you?"

"No, I guess not."

"I'll bet you didn't. But you sound like someone who knows a bargain when she sees it. Rennie, just give me your credit-card number, and I'll see to it that this revolutionary new system is shipped out to you today."

Rennie hesitates. "How much is it, again?"

"Just nineteen ninety-five, Rennie. Hard to believe, isn't it? Especially after what it's done for John Travolta."

"I'll take it."

"I though you would, Rennie. And it's the best decision you've ever made."

"John Travolta, huh?"

"That's right, Rennie. Just plug in your new right-brain augmentation system, and get ready to dance."

Rennie awakens slowly. Sunlight slips in around the window shades. Pigeons flutter on the roof. The sound of children comes up from the sidewalk.

Rennie starts to roll out of bed, then remembers the wires. She reaches up and untapes the electrodes from her head, puts them and the connecting wires on the night stand, and turns off the right-brain augmentation system. It's Saturday, she reminds herself, the day for a real test.

Following the instructions precisely, she doesn't waste time getting dressed. She doesn't eat breakfast. She doesn't even comb her hair. She gets up, walks to her desk, and sits down.

A piece of white paper lies on the desk in front of her, with the words "Mind Map" written at the top. A black, felt-tip pen sits beside the paper. Rennie closes her eyes, opens them slowly, and picks up the pen.

She draws a circle in the center of the page and waits for an idea to enter her mind. After a few seconds she writes the word "Poem" in the circle.

Next she extends a line out from the circle and draws another circle at the end. She stares at this new circle and waits for another idea. Nothing occurs. She waits awhile longer. Still nothing. Finally, she writes the word "Moon" in the circle.

From this circle, Rennie now draws another line and attaches another circle. She stares at the new circle, but nothing happens. She stares awhile longer. Nothing enters her mind. As she continues to stare, the circle begins to look like a cantaloupe. She tries to think of something else.

The cantaloupe breaks in two, and the right side starts to pulse with an orange glow. She tries to picture the moon. The right side of her cantaloupe grows larger and pulses faster, driving the moon from her thoughts. Nothing she tries can bring it back. She sighs, puts the pen down, and goes into the bathroom to take a shower.

Rennie stands in front of the mirror and sets her beret flat on her head. She has just read in *Art World Magazine* that "an artist should dress like an artist." But with her blond curls tumbling down on both the left side and the right, she can see that she looks more like Harpo Marx.

She tilts the cap to one side, then the other. She pushes it back on the crown of her head, then pulls it down in front. Every angle fails in one way or another. The expensive perm that makes her look just right for the office makes her look like a dope in a beret. She takes off the cap and puts it back into the drawer.

Twenty minutes later she walks into the La Vie de Bohème Café. In one corner a man with a black beard and a man with a pipe are playing chess. In the opposite corner a woman is alternately muttering to herself and chewing a pencil.

Rennie sits down at a small table and orders coffee and a croissant. The coffee tastes so strong that she almost drops the cup. She eats the croissant and opens her notebook. An article in the current issue of *Creativity Today* says that artists should seek inspiration by spending time in places frequented by other artists. Rennie gets out her pen and waits for lightning.

Across the room, the man with the beard moves one of his bishops and looks up. The man with the pipe stares at the board. Rennie positions the tip of her pen above the paper.

Five minutes later, the man with the pipe is still staring at the chessboard, and Rennie's pen is still poised above the unmarked paper. The man with the beard orders a cup of coffee. The woman in the opposite corner mutters and chews. Rennie puts down her pen.

Just as Rennie is starting to grow tired of this scene, Gina walks through the front door. "Hope I'm not late," she says.

"You're not," Rennie says. "I got here early."

"Writing something?" Gina says.

"Just a poem," Rennie says.

"Oh really? A poem. May I see it?"

"It's not coming out right. I threw away the first draft. I'll work on it later."

"Well, that's nice. That you're writing poetry. Is that why you wanted to come here?" She gestures at the room in general. The man with the pipe is still staring at the chessboard. The man with the beard is stirring his coffee. The woman has chewed her pencil almost in half.

"Yes, I guess so. You need the right atmosphere to be creative."

"I see what you mean." She looks at the woman with the pencil, then back at Rennie. "So how long have you been writing poetry?"

"Oh, for a while. I don't remember exactly."

"Have you sent anything out?"

"No, not yet. I'm still trying to find my own unique poetic voice." Rennie has read about discovering one's own unique poetic voice in *The Artist Within*, a recent book from New Horizons Press.

"You'll have to let me read some of your work someday."

"Sure. How about something to eat?"

They order lunch, and Rennie directs the conversation toward Gina's piano recital. Fifteen minutes later, the waitress arrives with their food.

Rennie looks around the room as the waitress arranges their dishes. The man with the pipe is still looking at the chessmen. The man with the beard has fallen asleep in his chair. The muttering woman has reduced her pencil to sawdust.

Gina picks up her sandwich and takes a bite. Rennie shoves the pen and the notebook into her bag and pushes it aside. Suddenly, she feels hungry. She picks up the knife, leans forward, and slices her stuffed tomato in half.

Rennie stands at the easel. She closes her eyes and pictures a ripe cantaloupe. She cuts it in two and separates the halves. She imagines the right half growing larger and beginning to pulse with an orange glow. She pushes the cantaloupe into the back of her thoughts and waits for inspiration.

Nothing happens. Rennie can't think of a thing to paint. What's worse, the left side of her cantaloupe starts to grow, and the right side becomes smaller. She tries to force the two halves back into their proper relationship. The right side is now no larger than the left and has stopped pulsing. The two halves move toward each other.

Rennie concentrates as hard as she can to keep the two halves apart. But now a moon appears in her imagination, and a fragment of poetry runs through her mind.

She forces the moon out of her thoughts and tries to keep the two halves of the cantaloupe apart. She imagines the right side growing larger, but the left side grows with it. The right half starts to pulse, but so does the left.

Rennie makes one last effort to control her cantaloupe, but with no success. It refuses to follow instructions. She finally gives up.

Now the two halves combine into one pulsating cantaloupe. The cantaloupe grows larger and fills Rennie's imagination with its orange glow. Then it slowly recedes into the back of her thoughts, leaving new openings in her consciousness.

New thoughts now begin to occupy these openings.

A painting forms in her mind. An entire sonnet appears. A short story writes itself.

A melody enters Rennie's imagination and fashions itself into a song. A mural appears on a wall. A novel—complete with plot, description, and characters—unfolds before her.

A sonata performs itself, followed by an entire symphony. Novels become trilogies. Trilogies become libraries.

Plays present themselves, with actors, scenery, and lighting. Films run without stopping, in color, in black and white. Couplets become quatrains. Quatrains become epics.

Rennie opens her eyes and looks out the window. The object she sees is no longer a tree. It's a **tree**. The animal on its branch is not a squirrel. It's a **squirrel**. Everything Rennie sees, she now sees in this new way.

Everything.

Chimneys, shingles, fire escapes. Windows, flower pots, air-conditioners. Streetlights, manhole covers, parking meters. Fireplugs, mailboxes, and garbage cans.

Rennie turns from the window and looks at the empty canvas. She hesitates a moment, then picks up a brush and begins to paint.

PATRICK NOLAND: HIS LIFE AND WORK

PATRICK NOLAND. His career spanned eighty years, during which he became the most popular literary figure of the post-modern era.

Born in Chicago in 1943, he grew up on the Southwest Side, where his father owned a successful mail-order business. His mother was a devoted homemaker and retired model. While Noland was still a boy, his father moved, at the request of the federal government, to Leavenworth, Kansas. Young Patrick didn't see his father for the next five-to-ten years, an experience that greatly influenced his later writing.

Noland's mother recognized his genius while he was still in diapers. His first word was "Daddy," and his first sentence was "Earn big money stuffing envelopes." While his father was living in Kansas, his mother resumed her modeling career, a decision celebrated in his first novel, *Silk and Leather*.

With his mother's encouragement, Patrick began to write while still in grade school. His use of graphic detail and earthy language frequently shocked his teachers, who initially tried to restrain him. They gave up this effort after the boy's mother spoke to his fourth-grade teacher in the compelling vernacular of the South State Street modeling establishments of that era.

Noland's first published story appeared in *True Story Digest* when he was only sixteen. Its opening is now a classic of the genre:

In his eagerness, Dirk ripped Veronica's dress into a pile of red rags. "Slowly, slowly," she whispered.

"I can't," he breathed.

"You must," she pleaded.

"I can't," he rebreathed.

Strong stuff.

During high school, Noland encountered more resistance from his English teachers. No matter what work they assigned, he submitted his latest piece of fiction, regardless of its content. This occasioned many dialogs with the assistant principal. Midway through his senior year, he dropped out.

At about the same time, Noland discovered mystery and suspense fiction, which gave his career a quantum leap in readership. Readers of *True Blood* magazine will never forget "Death at the Bus Depot":

The bullet left a little hole in Tony's chest and another the size of a volleyball when it exited his back. It caromed around the tiled room, made a small hole in his forehead and another the size of a softball in the back of his skull. It caromed around the room again and ...

More strong stuff.

When he reached his majority, Noland took his college degree from P.O. Box 1066, Bayonne, New Jersey. Thus credentialed, he left his childhood home to become the assistant director of the Iowa Bureau of Correspondence Study at Eastern Iowa University in Ottumwa.

Looking back, one can see the influence of his father in this fateful career move. Use of the mail had become a Noland tradition. He now had the support of a nurturing academic community. He began to write in earnest. Six weeks after Noland moved to Ottumwa, the director of the bureau was killed by a hit-and-run driver in a white Lincoln-Continental with white-sidewall tires.

Following this tragedy, Noland became the director of the Iowa Bureau of Correspondence Study. After assigning duties to his staff, he thereafter found time to devote himself more fully to literature, despite his many visits to P.O. Box 1588, where he practiced the entrepreneurial skills his father had taught him.

At this point in his career, Noland began to produce intergenerational novels with all the heft and substance for which that genre is known. *Mothers and Daughters and Fathers and Sons* is his best known, although *Cousins* received more critical acclaim and warrants an excerpt here:

> "Why, Rachel, why? Why in all those years didn't you write? You knew what our circumstances were. We needed you. We were counting on you. Why didn't you write or call or slip a note under the door or send word by someone? Anything to give us hope, to let us know that you were still alive, that you still cared, that we could still depend on you. Why, Rachel, why?"
>
> "I guess ..."
>
> "What?"
>
> "I ... I guess I don't know." Motes of dust fell through a ray of sunlight like the mist of an April morning. "I don't know," she repeated.

Noland quickly elevated this genre to the status of literature. During this period, he coined the phrase "insignificant other."

Throughout his career, Noland remained a mysterious and shadowy figure. At the Iowa Bureau of Correspondence Study, he rarely emerged from his office, preferring to remain at his desk, where he spent hours sorting and resorting piles of mailing labels. His colleagues eventually began referring to him as the "Ghost of the Labels." A co-worker recalls a conversation he had with Noland one hot July afternoon:

> Co-worker: Sure is hot.
>
> Noland: Sure is.
>
> Co-worker: Hard to concentrate when it's this hot.
>
> Noland: Real hard.
>
> Co-worker: They say the air-conditioning won't be fixed until October. It's going to be a long hot summer.
>
> Noland: Very long.

At this point, Noland disappeared into his office. The co-worker says he never had another conversation with the man, even though they worked in the same place for another five years.

It was during this shadowy period that Noland began to write horror fiction. The opening lines from *They Wake, They Walk* never grow stale:

> A ghostly figure rose from the mouth of the grave. It hovered above the ground for a moment, then swept through the air toward Jessica, who turned and ran screaming toward the car. "No, no!" she gasped. "Not me. Please, God, not me!"
>
> She clawed at the door handle, breaking two fingernails. She climbed in and frantically shoved the key into the ignition. She turned the key, the starter groaned, but the engine wouldn't start. Jessica looked at the dashboard. The gas gauge registered empty. She began to beat the steering wheel with her hands. "No, no, no!" she screamed. She beat the steering wheel until blood ran down her arms and soaked her white dress. Suddenly, the door swung open.

Clearly, this is not a book for the faint of heart.

After several years at the Iowa Bureau of Correspondence Study, Noland was forced to resign after a series of strange events in which his role was never made entirely clear. First, a huge pile of mailing labels disappeared during a false fire alarm. Next, a university administrator accused Noland of offering him a $5,000 bribe to move the bureau into the unused Magnetic Resonator Center, which commanded a superb view of the police station. Finally, Noland published a catalog of five hundred new courses for which he had no course materials and no instructors. When students began requesting refunds of their tuition for these courses, Noland refused to return a dime. All this occasioned a five-to-ten-year residence at a state facility in Fort Madison.

After leaving Fort Madison, Noland made his way to the Iowa Correspondence University in Des Moines, where he took a nonmanagerial position as a course writer and instructor. This move effected significant changes in his career. He married a woman twenty years younger than himself and fathered two children: Maria and Lucia. During these years he began writing inspirational literature. A sample from *Follow That Star* illustrates the depth of his thought in this period:

Do you feel rotten? Do you lack self-esteem? Do you think no one cares if you live or die? Do *you* care if you live or die? If you suffer from these negative thoughts, join the club. You're not alone. Everyone has self-doubts at one time or another, but some people do something about it while others continue to wallow in self-pity. The ones who do something succeed in life. The others do not.

What do the successful ones do? One thing, and one thing only. They change their attitude. If they can do it, so can you. They resolve to banish negative thoughts and think positively. They start whistling as soon as they wake up in the morning and continue throughout the day. One man I know even whistles while brushing his teeth. That's how confident he is.

As an indication of his own self-confidence, Noland published and marketed the book himself. The book would likely have brought him economic security had the Internal Revenue Service not become obsessed with ten thousand copies printed but unaccounted for in either Noland's inventory or sales figures. The subsequent fines and penalties left him in a weakened financial condition.

With this crisis, Noland returned to the gripping tales of love that had launched his career many years before. This, too, would have brought him financial success had it not been for the attacks of feminists, who now launched an all-out assault on Noland's entire *oeuvre*. These attacks initially boosted sales, but in the long run a well-organized boycott again brought him to the brink of financial ruin.

Still, in one of those inexplicable accidents of personal history, this episode had a therapeutic effect on Noland's psyche. He gave up all attempts to write commercially and began keeping a journal, which remained unpublished until after his death. He became a vegetarian and stopped using all stimulants. By living frugally, he and his family got by on his salary at the Iowa Correspondence University. His wife supplemented their income by selling duplicates of old photographs from her mother-in-law's modeling career, using P.O. Box 1929 in Des Moines.

As his memories of an unhappy past faded, Noland became less reclusive and began to explore the world around him. He spent weeks driving back and forth across the Central Plains in his white Lincoln-Continental with white-sidewall tires, stopping to take black-and-white photographs of abandoned towns and farmsteads. He copied the names of strangers from the tombstones of rural graveyards. He parked along country roads and spent hours staring at the horizon. He traveled the length of the Missouri River and hiked for days along abandoned railroads. Every year he took his children to watch the millions of migrating birds that stop along the Missouri River. He bought land in Nebraska and built a sod hut. He committed to memory the *Meditations* of Marcus Aurelius. When offered a managerial job, he turned it down. An excerpt from his journal reveals his mood at that time:

> Standing on the Great Plains, one can see the world and one's place in it with a clarity forever denied to those who live in a more varied terrain. In the emptiness of the Plains, mysticism is as natural as speech. The spirits of the dead hover above every spot of dirt. On the Great Plains, no one is ever alone.

> If you look past the apparent loneliness of the Plains, you'll see that this vast flatland is a living being. If you travel east from Denver into Iowa, the only elevation you'll see is the Loess Hills along the east bank of the Missouri River. Formed from billions of particles of windblown dust thousands of years ago, it is as if the Plains had removed one of its own ribs and laid it down as a reminder of itself.

As he grew older, his fascination with the Plains became more acute. He set out to photograph all the WPA murals in the post offices of Kansas and Nebraska. He inventoried all the windmills in Cherry County, Nebraska. In a spirit of community betterment, he started a rumor about earthquakes to scare all the tourists out of the Black Hills. He hired a street gang to collect and bury all the *USA Today* vending machines in Omaha. At his own expense, he reprinted thousands of copies of *Black Elk Speaks* and handed them out to strangers on the streets, in bus stations, and at railroad depots.

Noland lived well into the twenty-first century. His children grew, married, and prospered. Maria became the chairman of the board and chief executive officer of Sears, Roebuck and Company. Lucia became the postmaster general of the United States. Shortly before his death, after years of searching, Noland found the graves of his great-great-grandparents in a country cemetery in central Illinois. No one had tended the graveyard for years. From one end to the other, it was covered with prairie grass and wildflowers.

He died in Des Moines in 2043 at the age of 100, surrounded by his children and grandchildren. As death approached, he asked to be buried beside his great-great-grandparents. Room was left for his wife, who lived another ten years. On the last page of his journal, he wrote that he now believed the feminists had been correct in their criticism of his work and that he harbored no resentment against them. And beneath that, he wrote his own epitaph:

PATRICK NOLAND: DEAD WHITE MALE

BAR BISCUITS

Colin's stomach tightened as he approached the door. These meetings always made him wonder what had lured him into the ranks of Wisdom and Lowe, Inc. How had he—former student radical, editor of a short-lived literary journal, defender of the whale and the sea otter—ended up as a copywriter on the thirty-ninth floor of the John Hancock Building?

"Colin, how's it going?" Mr. Lowe said. "Come on in and have a seat. Be right with you."

Colin looked around the room while Mr. Lowe finished dictating a letter. The walls and shelves were littered with the relics of corporate life—pictures with the sales team in Vegas, unread books by Japanese businessmen, quotations by Vince Lombardi. Colin's head began to hurt.

Mr. Lowe swung his leather chair around facing Colin and leaned back with his little legs dangling toward the floor. "Colin," he said, "I want to talk to you about the Bar Biscuit account."

"Bar Biscuit?"

"That's right, Bar Biscuit. Brand new product. Brand new account. I'd like you to handle the whole thing from start to finish: literature, TV, the works. I think you're ready for something like this. What do you say?"

"Sure, I'm ready." He took a deep breath and rubbed the back of his neck.

"Good, Colin, good. I like your attitude. Very supportive." He leaned forward and clasped his hands like a television Baptist. "Let me tell you about Bar Biscuits. And let's keep this absolutely proprietary. You with me?" He peered intently at Colin's face.

"I'm with you."

"Excellent. I knew you'd understand." He sat back in the chair and assumed a scholarly tone. "Colin, Bar Biscuits are a revolutionary new snack food developed by the Better Bread Company specifically for the bar crowd." Colin tried to concentrate, but his mind began to wander. He pretended to take notes. "Bar Biscuits are salty like pretzels, crunchy like potato chips," Mr. Lowe continued. Colin looked out across Michigan Avenue as Mr. Lowe recited the characteristics of Bar Biscuits. Storm clouds were rolling in from the west.

"See what I mean?" Mr. Lowe said.

"Oh, yes," Colin said, turning away from the window. Mr. Lowe looked doubtful for a moment, then went on.

"Another terrific advantage of Bar Biscuits is that they come in two varieties: regular biscuits for regular beer drinkers, and light biscuits for light beer drinkers." He leaned forward and tapped the desk with his forefinger. "That's a real plus for people watching their weight."

"Right," Colin said, "a real plus." His head started to throb.

The sun disappeared behind a dark cloud, and a burst of thunder broke the afternoon stillness. Mr. Lowe was asserting the importance of weight control, and seemed not to notice. Colin flinched.

Mr. Lowe concluded his endorsement of Bar Biscuits and reached for a pile of photographs on the desk. "Here's a stack of glossies," he said. "They'll give you an idea what these biscuits look like. I'd like you to get together with Connie and figure out the best strategy from a psych angle."

Colin suddenly felt a new interest in the project. Connie Winchester, in his judgment, was the best-looking woman on the thirty-ninth floor. "That's about it," Mr. Lowe said. "Think about it over the weekend and get back to me Monday with an outline."

Colin made his escape and walked down the hall to Connie's office. The sign on the door said, "Constance Winchester, Ph.D., Director,

Psychometric Research. Knock before entering." He knocked. "Enter," a voice said.

"Connie, I need to talk to you about the Bar Biscuit account," Colin said, flipping to a clean page in his note pad. Connie stood up and walked around the desk. She was about five feet ten, and it had always seemed to Colin that most of her height consisted of legs—long, sensuous legs. He sat down and took out his pen.

"We just completed a study on Bar Biscuits here in the Chicago area," Connie said, picking up a stack of papers, "focusing on demographics and customer acceptance."

"Wonderful," Colin said. Connie's lips were full and ripe. Waves of dark brown hair broke over her shoulders.

She flipped through the papers and tossed them back onto the desk. "The study indicates a high degree of product acceptance among young college-educated males and females living in the north suburbs, excluding Skokie."

"Fascinating," Colin said. Connie's breasts rose like sand dunes.

"Blacks and Hispanics evinced a low level of acceptance, as did white men and women of all ages living in the south suburbs."

"Looks as if we'd better pitch it for the yuppies," Colin said.

"Exactly," Connie said. She pushed her hair back off her shoulders.

"Which media?"

"Slick magazines, the internet, and late-night TV. I wouldn't waste my time with newspapers and radio." She lifted her right leg and rested her hip on the edge of the desk. Colin looked at Connie's legs, made a series of random notes on his pad, and tried to think of another question.

"Billboards?" he ventured.

"Obviously not."

"What would be the best time of year to start the campaign?" he said.

"Early fall, after the resort season's over and everyone's back at work."

"You mean after everyone in Winnetka's back at work."

"Who else?" She stood up, walked to the window, and gazed up at the clouds.

"So Bar Biscuits won't make the summer hit parade in Cicero."

"I'm afraid not," she said without looking at him. "This is strictly a fall, winter, spring product for young executives-to-be. I'd pitch it with blue pin stripes and women's business suits. Anything else would be redundant."

"Redundant?" he said.

"Not efficacious, by virtue of irrelevance."

"No hungry hardhats wolfing down Bar Biscuits?" He hoped he wasn't trying too hard.

"Waste of money," she said as she turned around.

"And only with slick mags, the internet, and late-night TV."

"That's where you'll get the best bang for your buck." Colin wondered how he could get the best bang for his buck with Connie. "One other thing," she said, inspecting the floor with her blue-gray eyes.

"What's that?"

"The name."

"Yes?"

"Bar Biscuits. You'll have to get them to change it. Sounds too rural. No one will ever buy anything with a name like that." She crossed her arms and rubbed a spot on the carpet with the toe of her shoe. "When we called them 'Bar Biscuits,' the survey respondents wouldn't look at them. When we pitched them without any name at all, they ate them up, figuratively speaking. With a good name, they'll do even better." She took a copy of *Advertising Age* from a shelf and stared absently at the cover. "You need something trendy and up tempo, like the latest fad in French cuisine."

"How about 'Pain de Cabaret'?" he said, looking at her hopefully.

"Yeah, something like that." She dropped the magazine on a table, walked back to her desk, and rummaged through one of the drawers.

"Well," he said, "I think I've got enough to get started with." He closed his note pad and put the cap on his pen.

"Let me know if you need anything else." She sat down and began poking at the buttons on a hand calculator.

"Actually," he said, "it's almost five. How would you like to go somewhere later for a little Dubonnet and some Pain de Cabaret?" he said, staring at her.

She looked back at him and paused a moment. "I'd rather not get into a dating mode," she said.

"Dating mode?"

"I'd rather not."

Colin didn't bother going back to his desk. He took the elevator down and went out the door onto Michigan Avenue, stopping a moment to throw his note pad into a trash can. He walked to the corner and turned toward the State Street subway.

It started to rain. Hard. Colin buttoned his jacket and turned up the collar. He waited for the light at Rush Street, then leaned forward into the wind. The rain soaked his hair and streamed down his face. He began to run.

SELF-STARTER

Stormont glided through the dining room, followed by a party of four. He liked his job. He liked to open the menus, place them on the table, and motion to the waitress, the way they did it in the old Cary Grant movies. Stormont was the happiest employee at the Alpine Inn and Supper Club.

"Here we are, ladies and gentlemen," he said, pulling out a chair for the older of the two women.

"Thank you so much," she said, smiling up at Stormont's handsome face. Her own face was heavily powdered, and her gray hair had a mysterious blue tint.

"Your waitress will soon be here to serve you," Stormont said. He turned to summon the waitress and was disappointed to see her standing beside him with four glasses of water. He adjusted his Christian Dior tie, smoothed his wavy blond hair, and walked back to his station at the door.

The Alpine Inn and Supper Club stood just off Interstate 80 in central Nebraska. Stormont thought it the finest place in all the world, and it was his sole ambition to become its manager when Mr. Bergland retired. All he needed was a chance to show that he was management timber. The rest would be easy, like burning down the forest.

As he stood beside the cash register, contemplating his future, he saw Mr. Bergland approaching from the motel desk across the lobby. "How's the lunch crowd today, Storm?" Mr. Bergland said.

"Just great, Mr. Bergland. A monumentous crowd."

Mr. Bergland winced. He wanted nothing more than to send Stormont back to South Dakota, but the boy's good looks did seem to attract a well-heeled class of women to the Matterhorn Dining Room. "Good, Storm," he said. "Keep it up."

"I've been thinking of ways to enhance our menu capabilities. I'm keeping a list."

Mr. Bergland's mind began to wander. "Good for you, Storm," he said and retreated across the lobby.

Stormont had been trying to improve himself. Just the night before, he'd finished and mailed off lesson nine of Hotel and Motel Management—A Compleat Course. The letter that had arrived with the course materials said the program was geared toward self-starters. Stormont was a self-starter. No doubt about it. He thanked his lucky stars he'd sent in the coupon from that matchbook cover.

A woman and a little girl came through the front door and walked over to the dining room. "But I don't like it here," the girl said. "Why can't we go to Burger King?"

"That's about enough out of you," the woman said as Stormont recalled some of the main points in lesson four, "Dealing with the Weary Traveler." He stepped around a papier-mâché boulder and made ready to comfort the road-weary.

"Welcome to the Matterhorn Dining Room, madam. May I seat you?"

The woman stared vacantly at Stormont. "Do you have hamburgers?" she said.

"No, but we have ground-round burgers."

"That's good enough."

Stormont led them to a booth near the front of the room. On the wall was a plastic mosaic of an Alpine village, illuminated from behind by three fluorescent bulbs. It was Stormont's favorite work of art. It seemed to have a calming effect on weary travelers. "Would you like a booster chair for your infant child?" he said, remembering section two of lesson four.

"Naw," said the girl, clinging to the seat with both hands.

"Your waitress will soon be joining you," Stormont said, motioning to a waitress who had already disappeared into the kitchen.

About two-thirty, Mr. Bergland walked up to Stormont, who was placidly humming "Rocky Mountain High."

"Storm, I'm going downtown for a couple of hours," said Mr. Bergland, putting on a natty straw hat. The hat covered the bald part of his head, leaving exposed a terrace of gray hair that reached from temple to temple. "Talk to Alicia at the front desk if you need anything."

"Yes, sir, Mr. Bergland," Stormont said, the spell broken. He held the view that Alicia Conkwright was his chief rival at the Alpine Inn and Supper Club. She had graduated from the High Point Business Academy in Lincoln and was always finding ways to apply what she'd learned. "You can trust me in a crisis situation," Stormont said. "Everything is under observation."

Mr. Bergland shuddered, started to say something, then cut himself off and walked away. Stormont could see he'd made a good impression and busied himself with refilling the toothpick dispenser.

About ten minutes later, he finished with the toothpicks and began putting away the lunch menus and taking out the dinner menus. He'd been at it for several minutes when Alicia Conkwright approached from across the lobby.

"Hi, Storm," she said.

"Hello," Stormont said without looking up. He had somehow intermixed the lunch and dinner menus, and was struggling to repair the damage.

"Can I help you?"

"I'm perfectly able-bodied to do this myself," he said, looking at her for the first time. "Maybe you should just take care of the front desk."

"I only wanted to help. Why are you always so hostile?"

"I'm not hostile. I just have some negatory feelings towards you."

Alicia blinked, then went on. "Why do you have those feelings? I've always tried to be nice to you." Stormont didn't notice the affection in her dark eyes.

"You act like you know everything," he said, "just because you went to that college."

"I don't mean to be that way. I just want to be helpful. I'll try not to be so forward. Okay?"

"I guess so." Stormont could see that she was trying to trick him, but he had no intention of dropping his guard. His mother hadn't raised any dummies.

Alicia walked back to the front desk, and Stormont attacked the menu problem with renewed determination.

He had just got the menus sorted out and was dusting off the Hummels in the display case when he saw Alicia headed his way again, followed by two men in blue uniforms. "Who called the police?" he said.

"They're not policemen," Alicia said. "They're firemen, fire inspectors."

"Oh, well," he said, "nothing's burning here. Haven't had a fire in years. Sorry to've bothered you."

"They're not here for a fire. They just want to look for fire hazards. Could you show them through the kitchen? I have to get back to the desk."

Stormont's brain lunged into overdrive. He knew how to handle officialdom. "Right this way, officers," he said. The firemen followed him toward the kitchen.

"See, nothing wrong here," Stormont said, standing in the doorway so the firemen couldn't see past him.

"Would you let us by, please," the younger of the two men said. He was short and stocky, and wore his hair in a crew cut. "We can't see anything from out here."

"Whatever you insist," Stormont said, walking into the kitchen, where two middle-aged cooks in white dresses were preparing for the evening rush.

The firemen walked past Stormont and stopped in front of a large oven. The man with the crew cut opened the door and peered inside.

"Oh, there's nothing wrong with that," Stormont said, "nothing wrong in that oven."

"I didn't say anything *was* wrong. I'm just looking."

"Do you have a search warrant?" Stormont said, suddenly remembering a crucial section from lesson six, "You and the Law."

"We don't need a search warrant," said the fireman in annoyance. "We're just here for a routine fire inspection."

"But nothing's on fire," Stormont said triumphantly. "I demand my rights!"

The firemen brushed past him and continued on around the room. They checked the ovens, burners, vents, lights, cords, outlets, pipes, meters, motors, fuses, fans, garbage disposals, and storage cabinets.

They spent an hour doing what usually took ten minutes, with Stormont hounding them every step of the way.

"There, see, nothing burning in the whole place," Stormont said when they'd finished the inspection. "Nothing but the toast." He prided himself on his quick wit.

"You've got some minor infractions here we'd normally overlook," said the older of the two firemen as the other man filled out a form, "but for you we'll write them up."

The man with the crew cut tore a pink copy from a pad of forms and handed it to Stormont. "Take care of these things right away," he said. "We'll be back in two weeks for another look. If you haven't corrected everything, we'll take steps to see that you do. If you still won't comply, we'll shut you down."

"You can't do that," Stormont said. "This is the Alpine Inn and Supper Club."

The firemen walked out the door. Stormont stood there with the cooks gaping at him. "They won't get away with this," he said. He walked out of the kitchen, sailed through the dining room, and picked up the phone by the cash register.

"Dormer and Dormer," a female voice said.

"Hello," he said, "This is Stormont Blaine at the Alpine Inn and Supper Club. Our rights have been impacted. Let me speak to Mr. Dormer."

"Mr. Dormer, Senior, or Mr. Dormer, Junior?"

"Mr. Dormer, Senior. This is important."

"I'm sorry, but Mr. Dormer, Senior, is out of the office."

"Then let me speak to Mr. Dormer, Junior."

"I'm sorry, but Mr. Dormer, Junior, is out of the office. Would you like to leave a message?"

"Yes. Tell them to call as soon as they get back. We must take legal actions."

"I'll give them your message."

"Thank you for your reply," Stormont said and hung up the phone. There, he thought, that's taken care of. He walked across the lobby to the motel desk, stopping along the way to straighten the "Welcome, neighbor" sign in the hand of a wooden Swiss mountaineer.

Alicia was filing some papers when he reached the desk. He cleared his throat and drummed his fingers on the counter until she looked up.

"Hello," she said. "How'd it go with the fire inspectors?"

"Excellent. It could've been a very bad situation, but I know how to deal with people like that."

"Good."

"I just spoke to a young woman at Dormer and Dormer. I think we'll have to file suit."

Alicia's eyes widened.

"They can't push us around," he said.

Alicia's hands fell to her side.

"Send Mr. Bergland over as soon as he gets back," Stormont said. "I must go prepare for our dinner guests." He turned and walked majestically away.

Back at his post, he went over the things he wanted to say to Mr. Bergland. He'd begin by asking about his health, then move on to the health of his wife, his children, and all his grandchildren. Next, he'd report the episode with the firemen, dwelling on the importance of his own role. And once he'd set the mood, he'd skillfully change the subject; he even knew what words he'd use: "Mr. Bergland, I'd like to speak to you about my career trackage."

Who could refuse him now?

"Just give him one more chance," Alicia said. "If you fire him, it'll break his heart."

Mr. Bergland took off his glasses and rubbed the bridge of his nose. "The boy's an imbecile," he said. "I've got to get rid of him."

Alicia knew that Stormont wasn't very bright, but that hadn't made her any less infatuated with him. "Let me talk to him," she said. "I'll try to get him to use his head. I'll tell him he should think before he acts."

"He *can't* think. That's just the problem. He's an idiot. I've got to get him out of here before he destroys the place."

"Let me try."

"I've let you talk me out of it too many times already. Enough is enough."

"But he's so enthusiastic."

"Too enthusiastic if you ask me. Nothing's more dangerous than an enthusiastic idiot."

Alicia began to panic. If Stormont got fired, she'd never see him again. He wouldn't let her come near him. "Please, Mr. Bergland," she said, "Just one more chance. Let me talk to him."

Mr. Bergland put his elbows on the counter and rested his forehead on the palms of his hands. "I don't know why I'm even listening to you. You can't reason with him. His brain is too small."

"It won't hurt to try."

Mr. Bergland raised his head and looked at her. "This is absolutely the last time," he said. "One more incident like this and out he goes. Do you understand?"

"Yes."

"Once more and it's all over. He's driving me crazy."

"Don't worry. I'm sure I can do something with him," she said, although she didn't know what. "You won't be sorry."

Mr. Bergland didn't reply. He took a deep breath, picked up his hat, and walked into his office.

Alicia sat down and pretended to work on some room reservations, but she was really thinking about Stormont. He was very good looking, but terribly slow. It would be almost impossible to reason with him, especially since he already distrusted her.

She was so preoccupied with the problem that she didn't notice when Stormont walked up and leaned his slim figure against the counter. "Hello there," he said with a condescending smirk. "Did you see the look on Mr. Bergland's face when I told him about the fire officials?"

"Yes, I did," she said.

"He was obviously impressed with my crisis capabilities."

"Obviously." This was going to be harder than she'd expected.

"I had some other things I wanted to tell him, but he walked away before I had a chance. He was too joyous for words."

Alicia stood up and walked over to the counter.

"Stormont," she said, "I need to talk to you." She tried to appear casual, but her apprehension showed.

"Talk to me?"

"Yes."

"What about?" he said suspiciously.

"Oh, just things in general: the motel, the dining room, the way we do things."

"What about them?" His eyes narrowed as he stared at her.

She assumed a thoughtful expression. "I was just thinking how things seem to work out better when we think carefully before acting."

Stormont turned and gazed at the mirror on the door to the cloakroom. He adjusted his shirt sleeves until his cuffs extended exactly one-half inch beyond the sleeves of his jacket. "You're right about that," he said. Alicia felt a tremor of hope. "I always think very carefully before I do anything. That's how I keep from doing things wrong." Alicia's tremor subsided.

"What I mean," she said, "is that all of us make mistakes sometimes."

"Uh-huh."

"I make mistakes."

"Yes."

"Mr. Bergland makes mistakes."

"Uh-huh."

"Even you make mistakes."

He turned and glared at her. "When did I every make a mistake? You're trying to make me admit something I didn't do, but I won't do it. I've got my future in front of me."

"I'm not trying to get you to do anything," she said. "I just wanted to talk to you." She began to wonder if a handsome face was really all she wanted in a man.

"You don't want me to get Mr. Bergland's job," said Stormont. "You want it for yourself."

"You're missing the point."

"No, I'm not."

Absorbed in their disagreement, neither Alicia nor Stormont noticed the man, woman, and little boy standing at the counter. All three waited quietly for a moment. Then the woman said, "Excuse me."

"Good afternoon," said Alicia, reassuming her professional demeanor. The man and woman were wearing yellow T-shirts, on which the words "Old West Saloon—Casper, Wyoming" had been printed in blue. Both had on sunglasses. The boy wore a cowboy hat and had a toy revolver poking out of the holster on his belt. Stormont looked at the three people, then stepped away from the counter.

"We'd like a room for the night," the woman said.

"Just fill out this card, please," Alicia said, glancing at the directory behind her to see what rooms were available. When she looked back, she saw that Stormont had slipped behind the boy and was reaching for the toy pistol. He almost had it in his grasp, when suddenly the boy saw him and jumped away. Stormont lunged forward, and before Alicia could say anything, the two were wrestling for the gun.

"Gimme that," the boy said.

"Firearms are not allowed at the Alpine Inn and Supper Club," Stormont said. He always liked to help the guests amuse their children.

"Leave that boy alone!" the woman said.

"You must stop this criminal behavior at once," Stormont said. He pulled on the revolver while the boy held on with both hands.

"Stormont, stop that!" Alicia said. Mr. Bergland stepped out of his office to see what was going on.

"Let go of him!" the man said.

"We won't let you get away with this violation," Stormont said. He began prying the boy's fingers from the pistol.

"Stormont, what are you doing?" Mr. Bergland said.

Stormont kept pulling on the toy until the woman walked up to him and brought her hiking boot down violently on his foot. He let go and hopped over to a chair, moaning in pain. The man and woman hustled the boy toward the door. "You'll hear from our lawyer about this," the man shouted over his shoulder.

"We'd better call the police before someone gets hurt," Stormont said. "Those people are dangerous." He took off his shoe and began rubbing his foot.

"I don't think that'll be necessary," Mr. Bergland said. "Why don't you go lie down in one of the empty rooms and get that foot up."

"Good idea," Stormont said. He got up and limped through the small crowd that had gathered to investigate the commotion.

"All right, folks," he said. "Everything's under control. You can go back to your homes." He disappeared down a long hallway.

Alicia and Mr. Bergland looked at each other in amazement. "I'm going to get rid of him this time," Mr. Bergland said. "This is absolutely the last straw. He's got to go."

"I guess you're right," she said.

"If we don't get him out of here, he's going to ruin the place."

"I know," she sighed. "He's hopeless."

They stood in silence for a moment. Mr. Bergland was about to go call his lawyer, when Stormont came hobbling back into the lobby. "I called an ambulance. They said they'd be right out."

"Smart move, Storm," Mr. Bergland said. "Why don't you wait outside so you can get right into the ambulance and take off."

"Excellent idea." He limped out the door and sat down on a stone bench.

In a few minutes, the wail of a siren became audible. The sound rose and fell as the ambulance came down the highway and started up the long drive. Through the wide front window, Alicia and Mr. Bergland saw Stormont get up and walk to the curb. Sunlight fell on his shoulders, and a slight breeze tousled his hair. He stood there beside the driveway—his head erect, chest out, both arms in motion—directing traffic.

TAB AND TUI

Karen began backing the green VW into the parking space.

"You're getting too close to the curb," Mike said.

"No I'm not," Karen said.

"Yes you are," he said. "You're going to scrape the walls of the tires."

"You're just like an old woman," Karen said. "Worry, worry, worry." The tires scraped against the curb.

Mike got out of the car without a word. He stood on the sidewalk and looked at the tires. Then he shook his head from side to side.

"Come on," Karen said. "They'll be all right. Did you remember the race form?"

Mike shook his head a few more times, then reached into the car and retracted the race form from *The Dominion Post*.

"We already missed the first race at Wyndham," Karen said. "Now we're going to miss the first race at Masterton."

"Wanna bet?" Mike said.

At 1.63 meters tall, the trim and energetic Karen beat Mike's 1.73 meters across the finish line and into the TAB and Tui. As usual with these three-year-olds, the filly beat the colt. In addition to her trimness, the filly displayed angular features and a well-formed nose. For his part, the colt displayed an oval face and a large nose.

The TAB and Tui occupied a long, narrow room across the street from the abandoned post office. Along the right wall, a counter supported two cash registers, one for the purchase of beer, the other for the placing of bets. Two employees, a man with short gray hair and a woman with large green eyes, walked from place to place as needed. No one in the

TAB and Tui had any idea what "TAB" meant, except that it allowed them to bet on horse and dog races without going to a racetrack in Wanganui, New South Wales, or anyplace else.

Mike and Karen began the rigors of the afternoon by purchasing two mugs of Tui at $3.60 each. Then they mounted two stools at a long table and started examining the race form. They had already agreed to bet on all ten harness races at Wyndham, now reduced to nine because of Mike and Karen's late arrival, and all ten gallops at Masterton.

After arguing about the information on the race form, Karen and Mike looked up at the computer and television screens along the wall opposite the counter. Under the screen on the far left, the words "NEXT RACE" appeared on the wall. On the wall above the screen, someone had attached large photos of racehorses, jockeys, and drivers, but Karen and Mike paid no attention to them. They also paid no attention to the dog races.

Instead, they both looked at the television set in the center of the screens. The set showed the odds for the first race at Masterton. In the background, eight jockeys limbered up their eight thoroughbreds. A horse called Insider James led the odds in New Zealand, paying $1.30 to win.

"I say we bet a dollar on Insider James," Mike said.

"You always bet on the favorite," Karen said. "Why not bet on a long shot where you might make some real money?"

"Because Insider James has the best record, and because the favorite usually wins. That's why he's the favorite."

"All right, all right. That's what you always say. Make your bet before it's too late."

Mike walked over to the counter to bet his dollar. He could've used a betslip, but found that too complicated. Karen looked around the room. All the regulars were there—Maori men and women, European men and women, men and women who were part Maori and part European— a real melting pot of gambling addicts. Some people sat at the tables.

Others wandered about, looking at the screens and the racing statistics attached to the walls beneath the screens.

Mike placed his bet and came back to the table, where he and Karen sipped beer and watched the odds change. Insider James still led all others, now showing $1.20 to win. The jockeys rode their mounts toward the starting gate, where attendants began trying to get the horses in. As usual, all this took an agonizing length of time. Troy London, wearing the purple colors of Royal Stables, waited patiently atop Insider James.

Finally, all the horses had been pulled and shoved into the starting gate. "We're under starter's orders," the announcer said. The gate opened, and Insider James burst out like an artillery shell. "They're off and racing."

The horses reached the first turn. "It's Insider James leading by three lengths, with Desert Wind running second and Southern Cross running third," the announcer said.

"Why didn't you bet on Desert Wind to place?" Karen said.

"Always bet to win," Mike said. "You always bet to win."

"Troy London appears to be giving Insider James his head," the announcer said. Insider James led all horses into the last turn. "Here comes Desert Wind on the outside. He is gaining ground, but Insider James is running hard in front."

At the TAB and Tui, a brief outburst arose as the betters called out to their favorites. "Come on, come on," a woman shouted.

"At two hundred meters, Southern Cross is finding room on the inside," the announcer said. "Insider James is still running hard. And here comes Southern Cross as Samantha Doyle in the red colors waves the stick. Jim Houston is pushing Desert Wind on the outside. They're racing neck and neck for the lead. Insider James refuses to quit."

Inside the TAB and Tui, the noise had risen to a modest din. "Run, run," Mike called out. Even the two employees got excited.

The announcer's voice rose as if trying to be heard in the Tab and Tui. "At the post it's Southern Cross, Insider James, and Desert Wind."

"Rats," Mike said.

"Nice pick," Karen said.

After all nineteen races, they calculated their results: $19 wagered, $18 won, and $28.80 spent for eight mugs of Tui.

"Next time, I'll do the betting," Karen said.

The next afternoon, Karen collected twenty one-dollar coins. Each coin bore the image of a kiwi bird on one side and Queen Elizabeth II on the other side. The kiwi displayed a long, slender beak. The Queen did not.

"I'm betting on long shots every race," Karen said.

"That's twenty dollars down the toilet," Mike said.

For the first race, which came from Christchurch, Karen bet on King Tut, a trotter with the habit of breaking into a gallop. The driver, Paddy O'Keefe, struggled with the horse the entire race and managed to finish last, at which point King Tut was running with a slow but proper trot. Had the King finished first, he would have returned $30 for a $1 bet. But as it happened, he returned zero dollars regardless of the amount bet.

This race set a pattern, and Mike lost interest, choosing to spend his time buying beer and going to the toilet.

For Karen's eleventh race of the afternoon, a gallop from Hokitika on the South Island, Karen saw that Mike had again retreated into the gent's. She took that opportunity to reach into her purse and put ten dollars on Johnny B. Bad. The screen showed Johnny returning $90 to win, and Karen couldn't resist.

Karen was a woman of regular habits, not given to grand departures from reality. She put her money down calmly but obviously, having never before bet more than one dollar at a time. Word of this event spread throughout the room, and everyone became deranged.

The Dominion Post race form showed that Johnny B. Bad had made twenty starts for the year and had never finished first, second, or third. Johnny had earned nothing for Greensleeves Stables, and the word on the street was that the big gray three-year-old was destined for dog food.

Tracy Goodwin rode Johnny into the starting gate. Had the television camera focused on Tracy's face, it would have revealed a defeated aspect that jockeys don't often display. But at the TAB and Tui, the well-oiled betters ignored the horse's record, the jockey's face, and the drunken illusion that Johnny looked more like a kiwi bird than a racehorse.

In a field of eight horses, Johnny B. Bad left the gate dead last. The green colors worn by Tracy Goodwin stood out well, given that the closest horse was two lengths ahead at the first turn.

Johnny made up a little ground when he reached the back straight, and then a surprise occurred. A clod of something smelly flew from the right-rear hoof of Daddy's Boy and hit Tracy Goodwin full in the face. If Tracy had felt defeated before, the accidental impact of the clod changed her mood. She spat the stuff out, lowered her head, and raised her haunches. She gave Johnny two quick strokes of the stick, leaned forward, and said, "Go, Johnny, go."

Traci and Johnny smelled the track, the sweat, and the manure. They felt the impact of 545 kilos hitting the ground. Then Johnny B. Bad did something he'd never done before. He began to run as fast as he could.

Tracy steered Johnny around the last turn on the outside, where no clod would hit her in the face. With every gallop, Johnny gained ground on the leaders. Tracy rode like a madwoman. She wanted Johnny to get in front of all the other horses and jockeys and kick manure in their faces.

In Hokitika on the South Island, Johnny's challenge may have raised a shout or two. But Karen wasn't in Hokitika. She was in the TAB and Tui in the middle of the North Island, and everyone in the room was screaming for Tracy Goodwin and Johnny B. Bad.

Mike wasn't in the room with all the others. He was still in the gent's. He heard something, but couldn't tell what it was, not that he cared. All he wanted was another beer.

When he emerged from the toilet, he heard the sound of celebration but had no idea what had happened. Maybe somebody had just ordered free beer for everyone. Maybe the greyhounds had performed miracles in Auckland. Or maybe Parliament had abolished income taxes.

And when Mike walked back into the room and looked at the table, he couldn't help wondering where Karen had found all that money.

PATRICK IRELAN is the author of two family memoirs: *A Firefly in the Night* and *Central Standard: A Time, a Place, a Family*. His short stories and essays have appeared in a variety of journals and magazines. The short story "Reruns" was nominated for the Pushcart Prize. Irelan is the father of two daughters. He lives in Iowa.

The Ice Cube Press began publishing in 1993 to focus on how to best live with the natural world and to better understand how people can best live together in the communities they inhabit. Since this time, we've been recognized by a number of well-known writers, including Gary Snyder, Gene Logsdon, Wes Jackson, Patricia Hampl, Jim Harrison, Annie Dillard, Kathleen Norris, Michael Pollan, Janisse Ray, Alison Deming and Barry Lopez. We've published a number of well-known authors as well, including Mary Swander, Jim Heynen, Mary Pipher, Bill Holm, Carol Bly, Marvin Bell, Debra Marquart, Ted Kooser, Stephanie Mills, Bill McKibben and Paul Gruchow. Check out our books at our web site, with booksellers, or at museum shops, then discover why we are dedicated to "hearing the other side."

Ice Cube Press
205 N Front Street
North Liberty, Iowa 52317-9302
steve@icecubepress.com
www.icecubepress.com

outlandish waves of praise
over and over and over and over and over ...
to Fenna & Laura

ENVIRONMENTAL BENEFITS STATEMENT

Ice Cube Books saved the following resources by printing the pages of this book on chlorine free paper made with 100% post-consumer waste.

TREES	WATER	SOLID WASTE	GREENHOUSE GASES
2	**853**	**52**	**177**
FULLY GROWN	GALLONS	POUNDS	POUNDS

Calculations based on research by Environmental Defense and the Paper Task Force. Manufactured at Friesens Corporation